to receive a reply you must enclose a

S.A.S.E.

self-addressed stamped envelope

ARLENE SEIDEN LESHTZ

Lulu Press

This book is a fictionalized memoir. Names, incidents, characters and places may be the product of this author's imagination or are used fictitiously and may be in a different context. Any resemblance to actual events, locales, persons, living or dead are simply because I am a senior citizen, and my memory is slightly impaired. So, it may be just a coincidence, or then again, it may be true. Please take it with a "grain of salt" as the old saying goes...

Copyright © 2010 by Arlene Seiden Leshtz

Book Design by Aaron Leshtz
Edited and typed by Julie Leshtz Paritzky

ACKNOWLEDGEMENTS

I dedicate my book in loving memory of Archie, Mother, Dad, Grandma and Grandpa. There are many more who I remember often that touched my life and taught me so much.

I dedicate my book with love to my four children and seven grandchildren: Barry, Robert, Michael, Julie, Aaron, Ryan, Avital, Lilach, Shai, Hallel, and Idan, who are not obligated to read it (too much information about their Mom and Grandma!). To the kids who taught me how to email stuff; get things off the computer and all my endless questions over and over on how to do something. To my final "architect" who made it happen: you made this book a reality.

You know who you are, thank you, thank you! I love you ALL the same and to that one kid (strange but there seems to be more than one!) who keeps saying "I'm your favorite child" you know you are ALL my favorite!!!

Some special thank you's to so many of you who were there for me specifically with help on my book and over the years with my playwriting. Always with words of wisdom, with words of encouragement, my teachers, my weaver, my first readers, my honest 'critiquers,' my computer saviors, the typists and the listeners. I name you in no particular order, you know what parts you played: Donald, Julie, Sue, Dana, Reva, Celeste H., Lori, Ruthie L., Irene, Simmon, Chris, Bobbie B. Lisa D.

Best friends for their friendship, nieces (who make me feel like I'm the best "Auntie" ever) and anybody I might have missed, please forgive me.

Oh, and yes, I want to thank some of those "scumbags and liars" who gave me a few good chapters!

TABLE OF CONTENTS

My Name Is Anna...20

Early Halloween 26

Meeting Arthur..30

Excitement Of A Different Sort...36

My Father 42

How Do You Say No? 48

Another Way To Survive 54

Girlfriends 60

My Brother David..62

I'm Missing My Tonsils, My Appendix, One Kidney, Two
Breasts And One Earring Which I've Been Looking For Since
Last Week..66

Mark & Skippy...72

I Can't Swallow..78

Hannah And Ben 82

Scumbags And Liars 86

Depression 94

Saturdays.. 100

Larry, Pretend Husband.. 106

Israel, The No Fly Zone 112

Mother 128

Arthur / The Honeymoon 132

Book... 136

Epilogue.. 140

PROLOGUE

So how did I choose the title of my book? The following original correspondence between Ann Landers, a.k.a., Eppie Lederer, and myself will give you the answer. It was 1980 when I sent a letter and a large packet of samples to her. Here are just a very few of the actual samples I sent to Ann Landers.

March 2, 1981

Ann Landers
c/o Chicago Sun Times
401 N. Wabash
Chicago, Illinois 60611

Dear Ann:

On May 8, 1980 I mailed some material to you. The material
consisted of letters written to your column which I then
wrote answers to before reading your reply. I did this simply
as a pastime, never intending to show it to anyone. However,
I decided at that time to ask you to look at it and I also sent
a follow up letter a couple of months later. I have never had
a reply from you and of course was disappointed.

Here I go again! This time I'm enclosing a stamped, self-
addressed envelope (I think that may have been the original
problem) and I'm looking forward to hearing from you soon.

I know what a busy woman you are but I hope you'll take a few
minutes to read the enclosed material.

The only reason I have the nerve to show this to you is the fact
that since your life has changed in the last few years, (from
married to single etc., etc.), as mine has, I'm sure you find an
even deeper understanding (and you had plenty before!) of people,
as I do now since my life has so drastically changed. In other
words, "if you have walked the walk, it seems easier to talk the
talk."

I now feel a tremendous capacity for understanding and empathizing
with peoples' problems and for this reason I began to play this
little game with myself. The challenge was to read letters written
to you, keeping your answer covered, and then write my answer. The
fun part was comparing answers! I feel good about my writing and
the purpose of my sending it to you is to ask if you have any place
in your department where I might work with you in some capacity.

My life experiences in the past 6 years have been powerful and
I have personally grown tremendously. I have come from waking up
one morning a J.A.P.(Jewish American Princess), mother of 4, wife
of 23 years, to the next morning finding a "lump" in my breast, 10
days later having a bi-lateral mastectomy and 6 months later, very
suddenly my husband is dead. Next, my house is burglarized and on
and on. The things that always happened to "someone else" were
suddenly happening to me!

2

I'm sure you know, that "making it" as a single, middle-age woman is quite a challenge and I do feel as if I have been reborn.

I would love to hear from you. I decided to follow my intuition by sending the enclosed material and I guess this is what is called "chutzpah"!

Sincerely yours,

Arlene Lishtz

3

SHE'S SORRY SHE MARRIED A LOVER, NOT A DANCER

She's sorry she married a lover, not a dancer

Ann Landers

DEAR ANN LANDERS: Please tell your readers that a woman who loves to dance should marry a good dancer. I have always been crazy about dancing and made the mistake of marrying a lover, not a dancer. I thought I would be able to teach him how to dance AFTER we were married but I was dead wrong. The man has a tin ear. It is pure torture trying to get him to feel the beat of the music. (He also is tone deaf—couldn't carry a note with a co-signer.)

Every time we are around wonderful dance music, I get mad at myself. I could have taught him how to make love but I will never be able to teach him how to dance. Please, girls, don't make the same mistake I did
THEY'VE EITHER GOT IT
OR THEY HAVEN'T

DEAR EITHER: Sorry to disagree, dear, but I get many more complaints from women whose husbands are no good in bed than from those who are married to poor dancers. But thanks for writing.

Arlene's Answer:

Dear Either Or:

    It's a shame your husband "ain't got rhythm" on the dance floor — but - - I wouldn't discount that "rhythm" in bed! Hang in there or get into a dance class for yourself to release some of that energy.

SHE RESENTS HOLIDAY CARDS FROM DOGS, CATS

Dear Ann Landers:

I wonder if you get much correspondence from cats and dogs. At Christmas time we are 'honored' regularly by a wacky relative, but its never anything so lite as a manger scene or, heaven forbid, and Santa wreathed in holly. Instead, we receive a color snapshot of an ugly black cat perched on the TV, the piano, a cuckoo clock or the bathroom stool. It reads, "Holiday greetings from Boots and Family."

Another couple writes frequently. They sign their letters, "Bippy, Bill and Hattie." The dog, 'Bippie' always has to say hello whenever we talk on the long-distance telephone. Isn't that sweet?

We like animals and have had a good many, but none were smart enough to write or speak. Dear Ann Landers, where have we failed?

Is it possible for you to print this letter soon enough so those who are hard at work preparing their holiday masterpieces will leave us off their list this year? Please try

-Basic Betty in Phoenix

Ann Landers' Answer:

Dear Betty:

I'm typing as fast as I can. Sorry you didn't give me at least the first initial of your last name. There may be some Betty's in Phoenix who like to hear from cats, dogs, canaries, mountain lions, goldfish, raccoons and white mice.

Arlene's Answer:

Dear Betty:

I, too, have had a couple of animals in my lifetime and although one of my dogs could sing — she couldn't write. For some people their pets are truly a part of their family. As to having to talk to them on the phone, just politely decline.

SHE'S 19, WANTS TO MARRY MAN OF 44

Dear Ann Landers:

What advice do you have for a mature 19-year old woman who is planning to marry a man 44? The facts are these: John will have to pay child support for six more years. He also will have to pay alimony unless his wife remarries. (Slim chance — she's a real dog.)

John is in sales promotion. What is the average earning capacity for a man his age in that field? Is it likely to go up, or down?

If John should start another family, what are his chances of living to see his children through school?

If his health fails, could he be covered by insurance (taken out now) that would provide for his second family?

P.S.: John is a nice person, and I'm sure he is in love with me. I am....
UNDECIDED

Ann Landers' Answer:

Dear Undecided:

The faint praise with which you damned poor John in the postscript takes your problem out of the human relations category and puts it into the financial section. For his sake, as well as your, forget it, Toots.

Arlene's Answer:

Dear Undecided:

You don't seem the least undecided. You know what you want and it seems to have very little to do with love.

CHANGING A TIRE IN THE NAME OF EQUAL RIGHTS

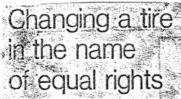

Dear Ann Landers:

There was a big discussion in the office today about Women's Lib and the equal rights amendment. How crazy can they get? One of the gals reported she was driving her husband to a fancy company stag dinner when they had a flat tire. She was in blue jeans and he was in his best suit.

He said "you change the tire, honey; I gotta keep myself looking spiffy." She did—while the big jerk sat in the car and listened to the radio. I almost swallowed my gum when I heard that one.

One of the anti-ERAers spoke up and said, "That's the way it ought to be. If women want to drive buses, trucks, taxis, planes, go to West Point and Annapolis, be firemen and mailmen, they should do everything men do—including changing tires on the car. They demand equal pay for equal work, and this, to me, means they want to be considered equals. So, in my opinion, they should get no breaks because of sex."

What do you think about this, Ann?

- Open ears and ready to listen

Ann Landers' Answer:

Dear Ears:

The situation you describe has nothing to do with the equal rights amendment (which I support), but it has a lot to do with common sense. Since hubby is in his best clothes and wifey is wearing jeans, she should give him a hand, to the best of her ability. But a lout who sits in the car listening to the radio while his wife changes a tire by herself deserves a foot — you know where.

Arlene's Answer:

Dear Open Ears:

It's good to know how to change a flat tire whether you're for ERA or not. As for the husband who didn't help change it, I agree he is a "big jerk."

Ann Landers
Field Newspaper Syndicate
Chicago Sun-Times Building
Chicago, Illinois 60611

March 5, 1981

Arlene Leshtz
3110 Pheasant Creek Drive
Northbrook, Illinois 60062

Dear Arlene Leshtz:

I received your letter of March 2nd, along with
your self-styled answers to letters that appear in my
column. You are really very able and have an unusual
flair for writing as well as keen insight.

This office has no record of your May 8, 1980
mailing. I am adamant about responding to mail. In
fact, downright compulsive. You would not believe the
number of letters directed to me that somehow get
lost. This goes for checks from me to others as well.

Please write again and tell me a little about
yourself. How old are you? Are you employed? Do
you want to be employed? Do you have young children
at home?

By now you have suspected that I have something in
mind. Well -- I do.

Next time you write to me, please write to my
home address. Chances for a letter reaching me
there are infinitely better.

I leave next week for Los Angeles and will be out
of the office for a few days, so do not despair if you
do not receive an immediate response to your letter.

Sincerely,

AL/km

12

March 9, 1981
Ann Landers
Field Newspaper Syndicate
Chicago Sun-Times
Chicago, Illinois

Dear Ann:

Thank you for your response of March .5th. I'm still "high" from receiving it and I appreciate your immediate answer and explanation.

You asked me to tell you a little about myself. In brief, I am a woman with 3 sons, and a daughter. At this time only my daughter and I live together.

I am a Chicago native and was always taken care of and brought up to believe that I always would be I left my parents' home, where my father worried about taking care of me, got married and then my husband took over the worries. I was happy being in the role of wife and particularly enjoyed being a mother. When suddenly in 1975 I was widowed, and 6 months earlier had just undergone a bi-lateral mastectomy surgery, I found I was now the one who had to worry.

After awhile, when my grieving had subsided enough for me to function fairly well, I gradually began to find out who I really was.

Some of my exposure to other experiences in my life had been as an actress and secretary, and many other things. However, always "for fun" never for the money. I emphasize this fact as it has played an important part in my life, as I struggled to support my family with my limited abilities for earning what I still call, "a man's living."

I feel I've come a long way - here's where I'm at now:

1. I work three days a week at a hospital as a Psych. Tech. where I administer a battery of neuro-psychological tests to patients who have suffered strokes, motor cycle accidents as well as other life threatening situations.

2. For many years I have been in training as a Transactional Analysis therapist and am working towards my clinical membership in the International Transactional Analysis Association.

3. I lead and coordinate "A Loss Group" which meets weekly at a local university.

4. I am a Volunteer Visitor for "Reach To Recovery" which is a program sponsored by the American Cancer Society.

5. I'm a student in a university where I'm working towards my degree in a masters candidate program.

Ann, you mentioned you have something in mind for me. I look forward, with great eagerness, to hearing from you so that we can discuss what this might be.

Thank you again for taking the time to read the material I sent you.

Sincerely,

Arlene Leshtz

Ann Landers
Field Newspaper Syndicate
Chicago Sun-Times Building
Chicago, Illinois 60611

March 10, 1981

Arlene Leshtz
3110 Pheasant Creek
Northbrook, Illinois 60062

Dear Arlene Leshtz:

Thank you for your immediate response to my letter. I
was pleased to hear from you.

Alas, what I had in mind was just a pipe dream, I fear.

I envisioned you as a person who might help me respond to
reader mail at home on your own trusty typewriter. This
would take considerable training, but I felt confident you
were literate, insightful, energetic and had a sense of
service as well as a high degree of compassion.

After reading your letter, however, I am certain you are
much too busy. Your life is filled with a variety of
activities that provide an income, the satisfaction of
volunteer services and the student aspect indicates that
what you really want to do is be an analyst.

I applaud your efforts and your energy -- quite a triumph
in the face of your recent physical problems.

So, dear, I wish you well and I do thank you for writing.

Sincerely,

Ann Landers

AL/km

March 13, 1981

Ann Landers
Field Newspaper Syndicate
Chicago Sun-Times Building
Chicago, Illinois

Dear Ann:

It seems that in my effort to "impress you" I gave you the wrong impression. I will try to explain more clearly. I am definitely interested in working with you and am certain that with a few changes I will have ample time. I am more than willing to make those changes.

Please be assured that I will not abuse the privilege of writing to you at your home address. However, I thank you for suggesting that I do.

I am looking for a better way to earn a living and am willing to change my job if there is a chance to earn the same, or perhaps more, and still do work I would feel good about. I would be proud to work for you and am certain I would do a good job after I was trained.

Yes, I do have an active life but all parts fit in very well and none would interfere with any work I might do for you. Also, I am flexible and would rearrange or give up what was necessary.

I hope you will reconsider having me as a person to help you respond to your mail. I would not undertake anything without giving my all to it, and I can assure you I will have the time to be a loyal, conscientious worker.

I do feel as if we've become pen pals! Seriously, I hope to hear from you again and thank you so much for taking time to respond to my letters.

Sincerely,

Arlene Leshtz

Ann Landers
Field Newspaper Syndicate
Chicago Sun-Times Building
Chicago, Illinois 60611

March 20, 1981

Arlene Leshtz
3110 Pheasant Creek Drive
Northbrook, Illinois 60062

Dear Arlene:

   Thanks for your letter of March 13th.

   I think you and I should meet and talk a little.

   I am doing a good bit of traveling these next several
days, but I will give you a call, or Kathy Mitchell, my
principal assistant will call to set up a mutually
convenient time.

   Forgive this hasty note, but I am running, running,
running.

                          Sincerely,

AL/km

17

She hired me!

I helped her respond to her readers' mail. I decided in my book the protagonist, Anna, would write to the "Answer Lady" my pseudonym for Ann Landers. The last sentence, to receive a reply you must enclose a self-addressed stamped envelope was at the bottom of her column and that was my final book title choice.

Being hired by Ann Landers reminded me of how resourceful I was in the past and now how I continue to be that woman who actually thought she could write a book. Thank you, Eppie Lederer, for giving me a chance to call myself a writer.

I am in the morning of my life every day and those things that I was "missing" do not define me. I have survived and I have thrived

CHAPTER 1

MY NAME IS ANNA

I saw him in a box. His eyes were closed and he wore a tallis around his shoulders. I know this because I gave his prayer shawl to somebody who asked me for it. I don't remember, maybe he was dressed in white. I don't know. It wasn't him. It was just something in there that looked like him.

I'm aware writing this I have a terrible pain in my chest.

I don't remember if I said anything at all while looking at my husband in the box. I just stared and thought what are you doing in there? Get out of there. Come on now just step out of there it's not Halloween. For God's sake, you can do it, just get out. What are you doing in that box? This isn't funny.

He was perfectly still. So quiet. So pale. I was really going crazy. I knew that for sure now.

*

Dear Answer Lady:

I can't seem to get back to life since my husband died. I feel like I'm drowning. I miss him.

-Still Sad in Chicago

Dear Still Sad:

It takes time to recover although you will never forget him. You will go through universal stages of mourning such as denial, anger, depression, anxiety and, finally, acceptance. Be patient, dear, take one day at a time.
-Answer Lady
(To receive a reply you must enclose a self-addressed stamped envelope)

*

On that last day, my husband's last day, it was a Sunday. Everything always seemed to happen on Sundays for me. The pastor or priest, he had on priest's clothing, said to me, "We did everything that we could." He took my hand, and I sensed something at that point. It was real, it wasn't my imagination anymore, something was very wrong. Why wouldn't they let me in the room to see him? I don't know what the pastor said. He took my hand again, and I pushed him away, I didn't want him to hold my hand, he felt like death. He repeated, "We did all we could," and said something about God. I never even heard what he said. I just knew I didn't want him to touch me or be near me.

The next thing I was aware of people were saying, "Give her something. Get her a tranquilizer."

I said, "I don't want anything, don't anybody touch me." They were all like vultures around me, I didn't want them around – I didn't want to hear what they were saying.

It seems that the next words I heard were, "Would it be all right if we did an autopsy? We need your permission."

What are you talking about? I want to see my husband, his name is Arthur. You're talking to the wrong person, you're mistaken, I'd like to see him now. You've got the wrong name, my husband's name is Arthur. He's in room 212, excuse me, I need to go to see my husband, please let me through, get out of my way, please.

"I'm sorry," someone said, again, but we need your permission for an autopsy."

"This is really getting out of hand, excuse me, but you are very confused," I said. "My husband is quite alive, you should certainly know that you can't do an autopsy on a person who is alive. I've got to call my brother. I've got to call my children please, please move out of my way."

No he wouldn't allow it, I do know that for sure, I thought. What is going on here, what is going on? I've got to call my children, and I realized at that instant that my daughter had been in that room where all my screaming was happening. Total hysteria. I remember begging them to get a doctor. Nobody listened.

I ran up to the desk saying, "Get a doctor, please, get a doctor," because there only seemed to be nurses running in and out of his room. "What's wrong, what's wrong?" I kept asking. If I can only get through writing this part, maybe I can go on, but I've got to get this over with. It's almost like reliving it and I'm nauseated just writing about it. The scream seems to still be in my throat. I feel very sick. I want to get the picture of that day out of my mind.

Now it was the next day. A funeral day. I got dressed, putting on that "little something" black dress and walked downstairs. A limousine was in front of our house. I remember coming back from the hospital the day Arthur died and suddenly throwing my purse, flinging it onto the grass and then running inside. So out of character for me, throwing things. I think the weather was beautiful, it was March. Oh, I don't know. I can't remember.

Oh, yes, I remember now. The day was perfect, warm and sunny. It was a perfect spring day. Whenever spring comes around, it used to be my favorite time of year, but now when it comes around, especially in those first few years, I was always sad, couldn't seem to enjoy the season.

We get into the limousine. Now it's myself and my children; our children. I believe my mother, my brother and his wife were with us in that car. My father wasn't there, he was recovering from surgery. I don't know why, but I felt guilty about not being a good mother.

Everybody took care of me and I couldn't even get to my children. My mother was always holding me. I don't know where my children are. I don't know, but I remember feeling I should be taking care of them, but how could I when I couldn't even stand up?

When we got to the door of the funeral home, somebody took us to a back room. Another parlor, a nice comfortable room, couches, lots of chairs, people all around. There are so many people already here. I saw Arthur's brother and sister, nieces and nephews, mostly his family pacing. It looked like everybody was pacing.

I said walking in the door, "What are we here for? We're not here for? What are we here for?" I wanted to say his name, but I couldn't say it. Somebody asked if I wanted to see him. It was somebody from the funeral home and somebody else. My mother was holding me constantly. I really didn't want her to hold me, and I couldn't get away, but she was always there, never ever letting me go.

But my mother was always determined. I remember how she smoked and when my youngest son said "Grandma, don't smoke anymore." She quit the same day. The night before I married Arthur she told me "don't ever say no to your husband for anything, just 'do it' whenever he wants you to." I learned from her all right. Now here I was and Arthur was in a coffin, what should I do Arthur?

Again, somebody asking if I wanted to see him, and I said, "Of course, I want to see him," and I literally ran. I don't know what else they said or if there were other people around. I don't know if I was alone. I just ran to him.

As the funeral service began, the Rabbi spoke. My body is limp. I have no spine. I can't keep my body erect. I keep slipping in the chair. I slither to the floor. Someone keeps pulling me back upright. I just want to stay on the ground.

I don't hear one word the Rabbi says. All I know is there is a box and my husband, my children's father is in it. I don't know what I'm doing here. I don't know what anyone is talking about. I'm being put into a car.

The kids and I don't say one word in the car. We drive somewhere. I get out of the car somehow. We sit again and something is said. We're in a tent. There is something white over our heads. It happens very fast. I can't stop them. I have words in my throat but I can't get them out in time.

"No. Don't put that thing in the ground." Before I know it's moving down and I have a scream stuck in my throat again. I let them put it in the ground. I can't stop them. I can't stop anything.

I turn around as we start to walk away. I turn to look back at the man who was my husband, the man I loved. One more time I want to see his face, hold his hand have him kiss me. All I see is someone turning the handle and the box go further down into the ground. Now I can't see the box anymore. That was it. It was gone – and so was he.

CHAPTER 2

EARLY HALLOWEEN

Mourning became an embarrassment. I would cry in the prune juice aisle so I just kept it to myself more and more. I just got on with life as best I could. I began to know my place. I learned to be careful at parties, with my friends' husbands – I'm not married anymore, the wives might think I was interested in them. Believe me, that was the last thing on my mind.

The "ghouls" came one night, unexpectedly. They called while I was out. The boys and my daughter were home. My nine year old daughter answered the phone. She was tricked by them. They didn't say exactly who they were or what they wanted.

They came over without having talked to me first and were there when I came home. "What is it you want?" I asked letting

26

them come into my house. They wanted to sell me a stone to put on the grave. They should have called first and talked to me.

The man was huge. His clothes were too tight. His pants were below his stomach. His wife was even bigger. "We're partners in the business," he said. "Do you know so and so? he asked in a coarse, loud voice.I wish I had been as assertive as I am now because I would have told them to get out of my house.

Somewhere along the way, I was supposed to have a stone put on the grave and then, a year or so later, go back to that place, where that box was put in the ground. We would say some prayers and the pain of it all would come back.

We would remember what had happened a year before. That's strange too, because the whole year is spent trying to forget. I spent the year trying to relieve the pain and then it's all brought back again.

We sat at the kitchen table. I didn't even want to bring them into the house. That's as far as I let them go. When they finally stopped talking and they talked a lot, they showed me a book and told me to look through it and pick a marker. I told them to pick anything. I didn't care what it looked like or what color it was.

"What do you want to say on it?" they asked. What did I want to say? I wanted to say get him out of there. He doesn't belong there. Instead, I told them his name and the year he was born and the year he died.

Then I said, also put on it, "our love forever." I remember later asking the children if there was anything they wanted inscribed on the stone. Somehow, we all agreed that the words, "our love forever," would work. We only had words, nothing else.

*

My mother amazed me over the years. She was a very kind, extraordinary, open-minded and unprejudiced woman. She was accepting of all different life styles. Uh, oh, sorry, I forgot. She was totally non-accepting of what she called fat people. Now, my father, well, that was another story.

My father, this bright, articulate, self-made man, owned a successful clothing manufacturing business. I hardly knew him. It seemed as if he was always reading, always hidden behind a newspaper, reading. Well, truth is, he couldn't read and he could barely write. Only my mother knew his secret. I remembered about his avoidance of funerals, even to those closest to him, but why, I wondered.

He didn't like old people, Jews, Gypsies, Gentiles, fat men with beards, short people, with or without beards, tall people, sick people, or red-heads. My father was a prejudiced man. It makes me ashamed. But he loved my brother, my mother and me.

My father was the youngest of twelve children growing up in Austria. I once tape-recorded his history:

"You were actually thrown out of your home, there were too many kids?" I asked.

"Yes, there were too many kids. There wasn't enough room. They said it's time to go."

"Your father wasn't unusual?"

"No, it happened to a lot of people in that stage of the game. You know how long ago I'm talking. I'm here almost 70 years; I'm talking about 75 years ago. I'm 80, maybe 90 now? When I was 5 years old, they chased me out of the house. They sent me across the way, where there was a tailor. I told you that already, a fellow that was in America once, and he got married, and he came back in that little town, and he opened up a sewing shop and they sent me to live, to learn the sewing business."

But, Dad, you were just a little kid! You were only 5 or 6 and they sent you away, sat you down at a sewing machine?

"I slept at home, but I went traveling with him at night. We went to other towns to sell his merchandise."

. I suppose there was a piece of my father in me, I sometimes used denial to get through things, and I knew I would regret it but something held me back. Now here I was, hardly a child, a woman with four children and no husband and a monument to select.

My mother told me a story about my father once, how, I was just born when the stock market crashed. He came to the hospital to see my mother and his new daughter, me Anna.

"Dearrre," he says, the endearing name he called my mother, "I lost all my money today. The market crashed – we're in a depression. The stocks are gone. We lost everything."

I lost my next meal as my mother "lost" her milk. I became a bottle fed baby from that moment on. I wonder if that was why I'm such a fussy eater. However, I only drink milk, not soda, not coffee, just milk. Any connection there, I wonder?

Denial, being taken care of and shock. It was still with me but now I had children to feed and a life to live.

CHAPTER 3

MEETING ARTHUR

Once, when I went to the cemetery I thought I knew where the grave was. I didn't. It took me a very long time to find it. I went in circles it seemed, the tears streaming down my face. Walking back and forth, up and down the aisles, always careful not to step on any other graves. It was foolish not to go to the office of the cemetery to ask for help, but I felt so ashamed to tell them, "I can't find my husband." I saw names on many gravestones of people I had known, a young man I had known in high school, a woman who had been married to a distant relative.

Finally, I accidentally found his gravesite. What was I supposed to do now? I only knew I wanted to talk to him, tell him about the children and how much we missed him. I didn't feel satisfied, only emotionally drained. I didn't return for many years.

*

When I met Arthur I was walking down the street carrying a box of thread to exchange it for a different color. I worked for my father in those days, one of my first jobs, and he sent me out to get the right colors, something that was done in the garment district.

This guy, this stranger. stopped me and says, "Who are you, who do you work for?" I was really taken aback because of the suddenness of the question. I answered "My name is Anna, I work for my father." I don't think he had time to answer or say anything because I just walked on realizing I had just stopped and talked to a stranger on the street.

A few days later this total stranger found a way to be introduced to me, becoming my husband six months later. I was young and innocent and now I was a married woman. I was determined to have children right away. He thought we should wait. A year later I was a mother. I won. And three more times I did it again.

I was so unprepared for marriage and children. My first shopping list after we were married consisted of caviar. Caviar! I thought every husband would love caviar. For what, I didn't know. As a matter of fact, I had never even tasted caviar. The next thing I did was open up a charge account at the local hardware store.

Now my husband was getting a little nervous, thinking maybe he had somebody on his hands who didn't know anything about money.

Years later, as I grew up, I was always amazed that I could make any important decisions by myself. When I bought a car alone, sold our house and traveled alone, it seemed as if it wasn't me doing it. It was a stranger, someone I was unfamiliar with, someone I absolutely didn't know, someone else was in my body.

Most everything not given away to charities I packed into one box and put into the basement. One box. A lifetime in one box! Navy dog tags, his yellow terrycloth bathrobe, (I just couldn't part with it, it was so him.) Letters from the years he was in the Navy, letters his father had meticulously saved. Many years later, I wrote a play using some of those over 200 letters.

What I did keep in his dresser drawer were his watch, cufflinks and eye glasses. For many years, I would find some small comfort in these items still being in his drawer. When the time was right for me to put them in the box I did.

He drank prune juice every morning so I always made sure I had it in the house for him. The children and I couldn't stand it. There were many foods I bought especially for my husband so even years later when I shopped, seeing a familiar food on the shelf would trigger a memory and might make me sad or remember a happy or funny incident about that item.

Prune juice, of course, was very important to him as the television commercials reminded us, it keeps you "regular" and we always laughed about this together.

He was fun. We played, in private. Whenever I was on the phone, he would do something funny, usually it was intimate, our own private jokes. I miss those moments. They were so much his and mine.

*

It was two years since Arthur had died. It was such a happy night. We were going to a party to celebrate my oldest son's engagement. We came home from the party, unlocked the door and we each went up to our bedroom. In one minute we ran downstairs to the living room telling what we saw in our own rooms.

A burglar had been in the house. My bedroom was the worst. Every drawer and every article in those drawers was strewn about the room. I felt naked. Someone had invaded my privacy.

The most surprising part of all was that the only items that appeared to have been stolen were two things, my gold wedding band and my small diamond engagement ring. True, I had no furs or expensive jewelry; however, it was eerie that these were the only items taken. And so, another piece of my former life died on that night.

The burglar must have been surprised. When the invader or invaders opened three of the drawers they found them empty, except for a large cardboard in each with a note written to me. My sister-in-law and best friend suspected that I would probably look in my husband's drawers shortly after I had disposed of his belongings. They had written on these cardboards and left one in each of the empty drawers in the hope the words would comfort me.

First cardboard: "If you need us just call."

Second cardboard: "Stay in the here and now."

Third cardboard, in the last drawer: "Things will get better."

*

Finally after three years we're moving in a week. I was able to make the decision to give up the house, our home for over twenty years. I couldn't keep it up financially so it forced me to move. One day there was a terrible rainstorm. The kind where when you read the newspaper headlines the next day, it says, "Sewers Back Up,"

"Storms Cause Severe Flooding," "Everybody Bailing Out," "Worst in Years." How true, oh, how true.

The worst part for me was taking away the security I wanted the children to have by coming back to our house; the house where they grew up. I have since learned that each one of the children, and this Mom, drive by whenever we have the chance, or when we want someone very important in our present lives to see it. Just a house, but packed with memories.

And yes, the boxes that were now packed, literally and figuratively. The fact that we were moving to much smaller living quarters meant I could keep only essentials and some of the past life. Many of those memories were packed in the basement in those boxes. The next day when I looked down and saw the boxes floating by in a foot of water all my life seemed to go by, too. The boxes began breaking up and softening. They were falling apart. So was I.

Yet, I was one of the lucky ones. I had a support system that was unsurpassed. My brother supported me emotionally and financially whenever he felt I needed it. No questions asked, just straight love and caring.

Parents who didn't know how to, but made every effort to take care of their "child" in their own way. Married friends, yes, some dropped off, however, the ones who stayed with me are still very dear to me. Special friends who never gave up on me endured my times of insanity and giving up. They held me up and persevered. My children kept wanting me to hang on, to be there for them, I knew that.

A totally different kind of support and strength was the discovery of how people, who had been resuscitated, supposedly brought back to life after considered clinically dead. This made death seem less frightening and kept me believing I was going to see him again someday. These people, in their retelling of the experience, made it seem peaceful and always saw their loved ones in a tunnel with light at the end of it. It worked for me.

How could I have done it differently? Oh, many ways, I'm sure now. It still bothers me that at the hospital on the day it happened, I simply screamed out when somebody there must have phoned the children "Your father's dead, your father is dead!" No warning, no understanding of their loss or their shock at hearing this horrendous news. I have no excuses, I was unaware of anything or anybody at that time. I simply had gone out of my mind.

CHAPTER 4

EXCITEMENT OF A DIFFERENT SORT

Dear Answer Lady:

Mother came to our house every Sunday when the children were young. She said, "Go take a nap, honey, I'll take care of them." And she did. She fed me peanut butter and jelly sandwiches when I was little. I fed mine a lot of that also. I wasn't so perfect either. Now here I am with no mother or father or husband and kids to feed. What do I do?

-Scared in Chicago

Dear Scared:

<u>*You need to move forward even though you are still grieving.*</u> *No one is coming to bail you out but you. We are stronger than we think we are. You'll see.*

> *-Answer Lady*
> *(to receive a reply you must enclose a self-addressed stamped envelope)*

I remember when the kids were getting older and we were driving to Disneyland. I had been packed for a week.

My husband hated to travel. An observant Jew he kept kosher so it was very hard for him to eat out and find food that was allowed. This lack of being able to travel was a big problem for us but, I so wanted to travel. We were ready to go – I had called the doctor when I got out of bed that morning. I found a small lump in my left breast and just thought he should know about it. Maybe schedule something for when we returned from Florida.

The phone rang as the kids piled into the car. I went to answer it and there was my Doctor's voice not yet so far away "I think you should come in now so we can take a look at that lump. Go to the Lab, I'll get the results from them."

"Ok. "I said." We're going off to Florida, haven't been on a vacation for many years, but I'll stop in your office as we drive by. Shouldn't take but a minute to look at it, right?"

And we did. "You probably have carcinoma insitu," the lab doctor said. Actually he didn't tell me right away. I was in the examining room after the needle biopsy, which unsuccessful or something about the test was going to be told to my Doctor. He and another doctor were talking about me it seemed.

"She's a friend of Bernie's. Her husband and Bernie were college roommates."

37

"So what," I thought, I overheard them talking about me?
Come on guys I have to get back to the kids, we're on our way to
Disneyland. They finally stopped talking at the barely open door
and walked in. I'm sure they wanted me to hear, they were getting
me ready for the big news.

"What is that" I asked? "What is carcinoma Insitu?"

"Cancer."

"What did you say?"

"You have to have a bilateral mastectomy."

"What's that? Both? Both what?"

"Both breasts need to be removed."

"What? What are you talking about? Why? There's nothing
wrong with me. I feel fine – the lump was benign you said. Why
both?" I took a deep breath, "am I going to die?"

"You can still go away and when you get back we'll do the
surgery."

"No. I don't want to wait. Do it fast. Will I be all right? What
will it look like – will it hurt? Why two? I never heard of two. Are
you sure, absolutely sure?"

I turned toward the door running out of the office toward
Arthur. Seeing me rush out of the office building Arthur got out of
the car and ran over to me. "Honey, I'm scared. Please help me.
Please don't let me go. Hold me."

For the first time in my life there was no self-consciousness
about being held in public. After leaving the doctor's office we
stayed together in the parking lot for a very long time. Judy opened
her car door and got out. She ran over to me "Mommy, what's
wrong?"

Bill hung back, probably sensing something, but Ron and Marty
stood awkward, all angles, leaning against the car.

Looking at Judy and the boys I looked up into Arthur's eyes
"Please don't let me die, I have so much to live for. The kids. Oh
my God."

I told the children to get into the car that we couldn't go to Disneyland right now because I had to have surgery. They wanted to know what kind and why and I told them. The car became quiet with the unknowing.

Arthur wanted me to see other doctors. I did. So many men looking, touching, pressing, thinking, answering, scaring me. It was so impersonal carrying pictures of my breasts from doctor to doctor, from hospital to hospital. So embarrassing and humiliating; I was scared. I saw the top men (I never did understand that, who decided who the "top men?" were). I went and went and went clutching my x-rays to my chest. We did this for ten days.

*

Both breasts were removed. My doctor, my friends and my family said "Wasn't I lucky – you're small, so small, no one will know the difference."

"You're a perfect candidate for reconstruction, we'll put implants in and you'll look great" the doctors said. After the surgery they sent me to plastic surgeons but I decided against it. I didn't want anything foreign in my body or want to cover up anything, just in case the cancer came back.

When I told Arthur he said "I'm scared, too, but you're not alone. We'll go through this together." He loved me. He held me. Funny, but we shared so many new feelings and it brought us even closer.

Newspaper headlines, TV broadcasts, magazine stories, radio broadcasts, every day, every hour, every headline – breast removed, breasts removed, the President of the United States of America's wife, Betty Ford, the Vice President's wife Happy Rockefeller had breasts removed too. Happy wasn't so happy. Hey, listen to me, me too, me too.

I hurt. Can't reach shelves, can't wash my hair, can't put my clothes on and can't take them off. The doctor says,

"Time. It will take a few months, that's all and you'll be fine. You'll be playing tennis in no time."

P.S. Doctor, I don't play tennis.

Finally I looked. I mean, really looked. I'm a freak. I'm mutilated. Please someone give me back my breasts. How will he stand it? I'll never let him see me. Never. Never again.

I want to get dressed, need a bra, old ones hurt, sink in. Special bras for mastectomy victims. There I said it.

"May I help you?" the saleslady said.

"Yes" I said (oh God I wish I could get out of here). I don't belong here. It's a dream. I did not have a mastectomy. I had two. Don't look so surprised. They all said I'll live. Don't worry. I won't die in the bra department. I have to go through the five year waiting period first.

"How much? You're kidding. Never mind. I'll try the regular bra section."

"No thank you I don't need any help I'll just try these on myself." The three-way mirror. Not good. Is this really me, trying to buy a brassier for no breasts? Who am I kidding? I've got to get out of here. I'll try another day when I'm feeling better.

First one in the family. Breast cancer. There I said that too. Daughter, please don't get it. They say it runs in families. Why did I start it? Mine's different though. Or is everybody lying? What's different? I don't understand it. What is carcinoma insitu? I go to the library. *Carcinoma: cancer; Insitu: in a given or original position.*

Ah. It hasn't moved or spread. So far so good. But they said it wasn't really cancer. What is it then? What is it? Husband, please tell me I'll be all right. I'm sorry to pressure you so much but you are so smart, so smart.

Does everybody know? I want the whole world to know. I want them to feel what I'm feeling.

Hey look at me. I don't have breasts. Oh God please no jokes about breasts and the almost total revealing of breasts. The really low-cut clothes. Sometimes I feel like I wasn't a real woman because I was so different. Still. I wanted people to know I'm ok even without breasts. In my heart I want others to know I'm a normal person. In my head I would think, please don't look at me and please know, please don't know. Please.

Many years later I would have six large screws and two rods after spinal fusion surgery. I am a bionic woman.

CHAPTER 5

MY FATHER

Dear Answer Lady:

My father is 97 years of age. I have always been embarrassed by him. He is a prejudiced man and has a nasty name for everyone: "Mr. W. has a long nose, Mrs. P. has hairy legs" and on and on. I want to know how he became so angry.

-Ashamed Daughter

_____

Dear Ashamed:

Ask him about his life before it is too late. We all have prejudices, not to excuse him, but to learn and understand him. I suspect it would be 97 interesting years.

Answer Lady
(to receive a reply you must enclose a self-addressed stamped envelope)

Dad, I want you to know how I feel sometimes. Sometimes I feel afraid like when you went into the hospital the same day Arthur did. Only you came home and he didn't. You had minor surgery, your first time in the hospital and yet you said nothing about my loss. And years later when I thought I might have needed a kidney transplant and I asked if you would give me one of yours, you answered, "it's too old, you wouldn't want it." That's not what I wanted to hear. It was another disappointment from my father.

Once I asked my Dad to let me learn to sew, like the women in his dress factory, like Aunt Sonya, my mother's sister knew how to do.

"No, you're my daughter, I won't allow you to become an operator at a sewing machine. You don't need to know how to sew." Oh, yes, I did need to know I thought much later on when I had all those children.

Once I tried. All on my own I got some material, looked at a pattern, and I made an absolutely beautiful, sheepskin winter jacket for my second son. It was really a gorgeous thing, he loved it, I was so proud of myself. He tried it on in front of the whole family and he has never forgotten it. Nor have I. Nor have his three other siblings.

It fit him perfectly, looked great. He was so excited and he showed how much he loved it. He strutted around the room, looking like a peacock, smiling and so were we all.

There seemed to be a problem. He really looked like a peacock, a very large bird with his wings outstretched, always outstretched because he could never lower them to land.

He tried to put his arms down and found he couldn't bend his arms. He had to keep his arms straight out and up, oh, my God, what had I done wrong? You see, Dad, I did need to learn to sew.

*

Once again my father told me his story:

"I was about ten or twelve, I don't know, and I went to this man, and I worked for him as a tailor. I learned the tailoring business. That's how I went into the dress business here because I understand tailoring. I worked for this man, and he used to have customers. He would make clothing for people in that little town, that town, Statchu, or Statcheen. I'll never forget it. It was right on the border of the Russian Volga, a river."

"So the last time you saw your father was when you left…?"

"No, he came, finally came to that little town, where I was. My father came to find out what I was doing, where I was at and I spoke to him, maybe five words and then he went over to my mother's brother, the one I told you about, the shechet. You remember what a shechet is? Not a butcher. He koshers the meat, cuts the necks off the chickens. He ignored me because they got me for $60 a year. This man was supposed to pay me for half a year $60, but he never did.

My uncle lived in that town with his two kids. In fact, one kid wrote to me here when the war broke out in Europe. We never heard from anyone in that family again, never."

Sometimes my father was a difficult man, but he loved his "Dearre" and his two children with a love that only a man who had very little love as a child was able to do. He learned and did what he was capable of doing and that didn't include flying even when years later he needed to fly.

When he was sick and couldn't walk anymore, something he had done everyday, he was angry. Big deal he was 90 he would say and frustrated with his aging body. Usually he walked from the north side of Chicago to downtown and he missed that walking. Not a big man his immediate world shrank matching his size.

Mother, ten years younger, couldn't lift him or take care of him anymore and he wouldn't let her out of his sight. He wouldn't let anyone else help her either. A neighbor tried to help coming over when mother sponged bathed him or needed to shop. He told her to "get out" and "go to hell."

I tried to help, my brother David tried and my father's face grew red waving us away and he almost told us the same thing he told the neighbor. We backed off but Mom's patience and strength finally gave out.

What to do now? David and I and my mother all told him we needed to take him to a hospital. Again he was angry but after we insisted he finally agreed. Another concession in a life full of concessions. This was a difficult decision for a man who never stayed overnight in a hospital, never went to a funeral and even missed his sister's and brother's funerals because he was afraid to fly.

He told me about his own father.

"Well, he wasn't always so mean, but he wasn't sweet as a father should be to a child but my mother was. I remember distinctly she once had to fight with him on account of me. The doctor told her to give me chicken soup, so you think I'm kidding? So she brought a little chicken and made some soup and gave it to me.

"My father didn't like the idea. 'Why give me chicken soup and not the others?' Well, I was a sick boy at that time. I don't know what was wrong with me. I didn't have color in my face…only the chicken soup brought me back to life and ever since that time I eat chicken soup. Your mother makes me chicken soup, and you make chicken soup just like she does. Yours is better than hers."

"Well, thank you Dad, but Mother makes good soup, maybe you could tell her that, too," I casually suggested. He, however, just went right on with his story.

"Anyway, the story at the end is when I went to Berlin and I met my uncle, my father's brother. He had four children all in the egg business in Berlin. At that time the egg business was a terrific business. They had bins in the store they owned. In the bins were bunches of eggs laid out. I don't know, five cents a dozen, six cents a dozen. My uncle was also married a second time. She was a German woman, a beautiful, fine woman. She used to come over and bring eggs to the people I worked for to show appreciation that I had a job. Such a nice woman. She had a son; I stayed with her even after my uncle died. He died six months after I was in Berlin. And I lived with her, such a sweet person, a wonderful person. She's left with one child. The other children were from his first wife. Do you understand? She was a widow with one child.

"I had a job with a tailor making men's suits. I used to sew in sleeves in jackets for men's jackets. Beautiful place. At that time, a big place, electric machines already – and that's where I ended up. Then we had a strike.

"Somebody started a fire, I ran and kept running, I was just a kid, I was so scared, and the flames were so hot. Someone hollered, 'we're all going to hell.' I remember a guy came in counting how many people the tailor had working for him and he stopped at the door. He yelled something in German telling us to get out of there. 'Arbeitet hier?' he yelled, pushing himself in the door. 'Who works here?' He counted me and about three other guys who didn't belong to the union. We were scabs.

"I'd work during the day, and she used to give me sandwiches. She used to make me sandwiches, this aunt."

He was a proud, fearful man who learned the manufacturing business and built a successful company making women's dresses. The 'burning in hell' memory from his childhood in Berlin, contributed to his being frightened out of his mind of dying. Now in his nineties, his world shrinking we took him to a nursing home and not a hospital but he never let on that he knew it wasn't a hospital.

He didn't know what a nursing home was like so I really don't think he knew where he was. He wouldn't have liked that. He often said he didn't want to be with "old" people.

He died within two days after coming to the nursing home. He had a cerebral vascular attack, in other words, a stroke leaving him unable to talk. In those last two days, his eyes were always watering.

Of course, those were tears which he couldn't talk about and probably wouldn't have even if he could talk. There they were my mother bending over my father taking care of him as she had done for sixty-seven years.. She held his hand in her frail hand. She kissed his cheek and they looked into each other's eyes searching the other's eyes. My mother took a tissue, folded it and wiped his tears away. She said "it's ok Jacob, I'm ok." She sat on the plastic chair next to the bed sometimes putting her head rimmed with its still dark-dyed hair on his arm. Dad still wouldn't let her go gray – "I don't want an old woman for a wife," he said. His arm trembled in response. In the end he wasn't alone finally accepting the comfort of each other's love until he had his last breath. We had the words, "he loved us" put on his tombstone. He was my father. I loved him.

CHAPTER 6

HOW DO YOU SAY NO?

My mother, Sarah, was 96 when she realized she couldn't be everything to everybody. I learned it sooner than that.

She made many adjustments in her life always with a positive attitude; especially when she lived in half of a tiny room the size of a large walk-in closet sharing it with another nursing home resident. Each new roommate became a new marriage. Nicknamed "Lady Sarah" by the other nursing home residents and staff, now with her white hair, she looked like 'aristocracy.' See what you missed Dad?

Mother smoked cigarettes but when my youngest son said "Grandma don't smoke anymore," she stopped that same day. I couldn't quit when my kids begged me to stop. She was determined.

If I wanted to go with David, and I always did, she said, "Take Anna with you." He did. She never told me anything about life. She told David to do that. He did. Oh yes. I learned from her alright. It took me many years of life to learn who I was and that it was also okay to say no sometimes. Mother had to wait until she was 96 to learn to say no. I didn't.

*

She told me about Maria her current roommate.

Maria was an 83 year old woman, whose native language was Spanish. She was hyperactive, constantly moving and walking. She hardly ever stopped moving. My mother would drop her voice when I came to visit her motioning me over so she could whisper in my ear, "I think Maria suffers from the early stages of dementia," looking around to make sure Maria couldn't hear, "I've heard the doctors say she's paranoid." Then she would nod and shake her head. One day when Maria wasn't around, she went on to tell me about her.

"We're in our room, I sat up in bed very quickly disoriented because Maria's TV suddenly went on and it scared me to death. 'Please, Maria, turn down your television. It's very late. I can't sleep.'

She didn't answer me. She turned her back to me. 'Maria, you're hard of hearing, please put your hearing aids in, now.' She wouldn't answer. I jumped out of bed, got my walker because it was dark in the room, and I went over to her bed. 'I asked you to put your hearing aids in. Did you hear me? I can't stand it anymore. Answer me, Maria. Look at me, it's me, Sarah. Why won't you talk to me?"

'Leave me alone,' Maria said.

'I'm calling for help. You're a crazy lady. I can't understand what I've done, why don't you talk to me?' And the next thing I know she gets up, goes to the TV set and suddenly pulls the plug out of the wall, picks up the set and puts it on my bed! I scream and break down crying."

"And another night," mother tells me, "I'm sleeping again. I open my eyes and Maria is standing over me climbing on to my bed. She's shaking her fingers and holding her hand out in front of my face. She's speaking Spanish and English, speaking very quickly and asking me for money.

'Wake up, give me money, I need money,' she yelled at me.

'I don't have any money! Leave me alone!' I said, 'I'm an old woman, I'm a woman who has never had a fight, people love me. What have I ever done to you? Why don't you like me? Why are you so mean?'

"I told her that you and David said she's sick and she can't help herself. David is very smart (oh, how I wanted mother to say that I was very smart too, but, I was 'just' a girl and never could be as smart as my brother, David) and David said, 'there's something wrong with her mind' and that it has nothing to do with me."

Later on in my parenting years, I remember my daughter saying something very much the same to me. "Mom, why do you always ask my brothers to fix things? I know how and I'm just as good at it as they are." I'm sure I answered, 'but you're a girl.' Again, the apple doesn't fall far from the tree. I've tried not to make that same mistake with her again. However, it still sneaks out of my mouth occasionally.

I thought as I listened to Mother's story, another thing I learned, I also thought everybody had to like me. Now, at least I know where I had learned it. I'm better now.

In those last years my mother stopped biting her lower lip to stop from saying what she thought or wanted to say. It sure confused me. About Maria she said "tell me why she doesn't like me, I'm a good person." I didn't know who she was those last years. We were still the luckiest people in that entire nursing home. These changes were only evident to David and me and a few of the grandkids. One grandson once commented that Nonny (the grandkids call her that) is an "imposter!" To others who visited or loved her they never saw anything like what we saw at times.

She played poker, sang in the Glee Club and went to the Bible study class. My Jewish mother sometimes went to Rosary with her girl friends in the retirement home. She went to exercise classes, lectures, played bingo and always asked "what's for lunch?" And when chewing her last bite of lunch would wonder aloud "what's for dinner?"

Oh my God, the retirement home; the wonder and the curse of it. She didn't want to go even after her bout of colon cancer at age 93, then came the broken hip and a slight stroke so David and I convinced her to move for her own safety. She adapted as she always did.

Never again did I have one of her famous brownies, barbequed brisket, cucumbers marinated in vinegar and sugar, sour cream coffee cake, salmon patties, cream cheese jelly cookies, cheese blintzes or lemon meringue pie. No. She never baked or cooked again.

I lost my mother but she found herself. I applaud the change for her. I cry for myself. It takes her longer to answer the phone now. She still calls me every day or I call her. This was about the only thing she ever really wanted me to do, I did it.

She doesn't say yes to everything. She doesn't look at me when talking – she looks at everyone else. She doesn't even like everybody and gossips and complains sometimes.

I lost my old mother. You can stop holding your mouth so tight now. It's ok to be angry. It's ok, Mom, I do understand. It's just that I'm such a baby about it. I want my other mother back and it does make me ashamed to feel like this.

51

I don't get birthday cards anymore and no small check every year. I'm now the one sending cards as if from Mother to others and writing checks to put in with the cards.

Here's what they used to sound like when she picked the cards herself, and always wrote something very special, she was much better at that than I am.

*

Anna "Dearest" Best Friend and Daughter –

Happy Birthday!!!

It's hard to believe that so many years ago, I gave birth to you. Where did the years go? How fortunate I am to have learned so much from you and David. I am a very lucky mother!! I wish I could express myself better – but I am doing the best I can! It just comes naturally for you to care about other people. I am so proud of you! Good luck and good health for the rest of your life and I wish you the best of everything you want to accomplish.

-Love, Mom

Dear Anna,

You have such a wonderful heart, the helpful things you say and do for me and care for me. If it wasn't for you, I wouldn't be where I am! I am a lucky person.

Having you and David has been a blessing to me. I can never tell you enough!!!!!

God bless you and keep you. Happy Birthday!
Love & kisses,

-Mother

*

I thought as I re-read the letters and cards, lots of exclamation points, she was that kind of mother! (Oops! Me, too!!!!)

CHAPTER 7

ANOTHER WAY TO SURVIVE

And so now it begins. I'm forty-four years old. I am a widow with four children, three sons and a daughter. My husband Arthur died suddenly after we had been married for almost twenty-three years. Six months before he died, I was diagnosed with breast cancer. I thought I was going to die. He beat me.

I'm a Chicago native and a past "Jewish American Princess." I was always taken care of and was brought up to believe that I always would be. I left my parents, Jacob and Sarah's home, where my father worried about taking care of my mother, brother and me. Arthur said, "I worry about the money you take care of the house and the kids. Okay?"

"Okay," I said.

I was happy being in the role of wife and particularly enjoyed being a mother. I never had a worry that Arthur didn't take care of. He got the ulcers, I got a great husband.

*

When I was 17 my picture is listed in the Chicago Talent Directory for Radio, Television, Movies, and Modeling the "bible" of the industry at that time.

> Anna, phone: DE7-7334,
> Age: 17
> Voice range: 12 to 19.
> Adolescents and any type teen.
> Emotionals: (yep, that's what they called it in those days, we weren't into Stanislavski type acting yet) comedy, ingénues, experienced in Coronet pictures, television, radio and stage.

I continued to be involved in theater as an adult. I was in "All The King's Men," "Look Homeward Angel," almost all the Tennessee Williams plays and so many more I can't remember. When I was about 5 months pregnant with my second child, I played a 16 year old in "The Crucible," by Arthur Miller.

Obviously, I was not showing yet. I only gained 13 pounds when I delivered my son. I became a good actress, because I lived and experienced real life although not always the easy life. I even became a member of the Screen Actor's Guild. I never got much more than the SAG card, a few commercials and some walk on parts as an extra in a handful of films as well. It was a little too competitive for this shy girl.

After I was married, I performed in local theater groups, amateur and professional as an outlet. I had some success, in that when I auditioned for a role in a play, I usually would get a part. My husband tolerated this. He was proud of me. However he didn't like the demands it put upon my time. Sometimes he just wanted me there with him even when he changed a light bulb. I was loved. Oh, yes, he loved me.

I continued with my education by attending Adult Education classes, lectures, workshops and seminars, mostly for my own enrichment and not for college credit, all the time being a devoted wife and mother.

After Arthur was gone, it took me many years but I finally graduated from college at age fifty-two. I was smart and I began to believe it. I was so traumatized and convinced that "girls aren't supposed to be smart" that when I learned I had to take a statistics course, I was ready to quit. I was not a wizard at numbers. My fourth grade teacher was an alcoholic and never taught me or anyone else in the class anything and it was the year of arithmetic. The school staff didn't notice this absentee teacher and it was my first experience with "doodling," on those days when he was slurring his words.

Now I needed to take statistics in order to graduate with a degree in psychology. This was the end for me, I knew. Then the professor took me on as his special project and promised that I could learn and that I would pass. His only requirement was that I ask questions. Any and all questions, stupid ones especially. I did that and I was smart. I passed. Got a B. Okay, so it wasn't an A, but don't forget, I was only a girl.

My one regret was that I didn't participate in the graduation ceremonies. I thought I was too old and the children would be embarrassed by this older woman wearing a cap and gown, graduating from college. How wrong I was, they would have been so proud.

*

"Arthur did you see this book?" I asked.

"What book?"

"The book on Transactional Analysis. They call it TA. I think we can maybe save your brother's marriage with this book. Maybe even become TA therapists."

So we became therapists. We studied about Eric Berne, M.D. the founder of TA. We read Thomas A. Harris's, "I'm Ok- You're Ok." And, after Arthur was gone, I studied for eight more years. Of course, it didn't save Arthur's brother's marriage because we forgot to ask "do you want to change?" He didn't. I, on the other hand, stopped smoking forever when I finally made up my mind to do it. He wasn't at all like

me.

This was a turning point in our lives. We both began to change and our marriage now improved even more by leaps and bounds. Arthur was always late. I was always early. We talked and talked. Why? What triggered the problems we had because of it? T.A. helped us to solve it by learning why.

OK, so Arthur's mother, who called him "Arthuralleh" a loving name, hard to say, but she did it only when angry – so it left its mark on him. "Hurry up, Arthuralleh, we'll be late. You're so slow, hurry, hurry, hurry."

So Arthuralleh chose to rebel when my voice sounded a little bit like his mother's. So, now, thanks to what we learned from TA, he could be late and I could be early.

There were even times when we left for events at different times. It worked. Our differences became "okay." Separateness didn't mean we didn't love one another.

I stopped playing a favorite game of mine, which the psychotherapist Eric Berne, called "Kick Me." My husband stopped some of his old games and we became more honest and intimate with one another. I took to T.A. as a "duck takes to water."

Things went along very well for my family and me. I worked one day a week, on Saturdays at a counseling agency for eight years; all I knew how to do was type. My husband encouraged me as he felt the experience would be good for me "if anything ever happened to me and you had to work," he said. (Maybe he might have had a premonition?)

He was always home on Saturdays because he observed the Jewish Sabbath. Sometimes with some guilt because he wasn't at work on that day earning a living for us. I worked for fun, not for the money as the amount I earned was minimal.

Besides I usually spent more on getting there and on my lunch than I earned. Always needed the whole shebang: an appetizer, usually tomato juice, with crackers and butter, the meat, usually a hamburger, well done, a potato, French fries, of course, salad, with thousand island dressing, a roll or white bread, and at least two pats of butter. No dessert, I was too full by then. And I still only weighed about ninety nine pounds. Okay, I'm ready to admit I had some weird food habits.

Giving my all I discovered I worked well and had empathy for the clients and their problems. I loved typing the case histories and looked forward to coming in week after week in order to follow the stories of the people involved.

I had worked in other jobs as a teenager, selling in a retail department store and working for my father in his manufacturing business, always for fun, never for the money. I emphasize this fact, as it plays a tremendous part in my life as I struggled to support my family with my limited abilities for earning what I still call "a man's living."

S.A.S.E.

CHAPTER 8

GIRLFRIENDS

"Hi how are you? Where have you been? Are you okay?"

"I'm fine. No, wait. I'm not" I said to my girlfriend, Donna. "I know. It's just that I attended this funeral yesterday and the first words out of my mouth to the new widow were "how are you?"

"Yeah. I know. Everyone always asks me the same thing."

"So. How are you?" I said giggling a little at the absurdity of it.

"Fine" Donna said. "Just fine."

It isn't that we don't care. Sometimes we're so involved in our own lives that if we really heard what the other person had to say we probably wouldn't know what to do or say. That's just too much responsibility.

Donna and I talked and talked for many years. We cried together. We laughed together. We confided secrets and we told the truth. We talked about our husbands, current and deceased, the almost ones, the good ones, the bad ones, our kids, our parents, our work, our play and our health.

We just kept talking and we sometimes solved our problems. Sometimes we just listened to one another as we walked on our crooked paths. Thank God for girlfriends.

"I'm reading a book about love. It says some of our happiest moments come from the time before we're born, when we're still in the womb. I wonder if that's what I'm remembering when, out of the blue, I have a sudden surge of happiness. Has that ever happened to you?" Donna asked.

"Sometimes," I said, thinking back on my life. "Sometimes."

CHAPTER 9

MY BROTHER DAVID

We talked about our brothers.

My hero was my brother David. I adored him. Once I had a dream where David told me: "When I was 2-1/2 years old you were born. I had a baby sister. My responsibility for you started at this very tender age. I look back on a family picture of me and I can see the burden written on my face. Mother assigned you to me."

"Take care of your little sister" she said "teach her everything. I'm very busy. I don't know how to do it" she told me "I have to take care of your father." David went on: "as I grew up you were my little shadow. As we grew older, every Saturday I took you to the movies. Every day I bought you tootsie rolls that you devoured. Then to the playground pushing your swing."

"Later I watched you play roly-poly bouncing the ball into the squares drawn on the sidewalk, you were good, you played jacks, those little metal pieces you threw down and then tried to pick up. All those games you played with your girlfriends. And to this day I want you to know I'm still here to take care of you. There were times when I didn't want to take you and I was angry but at the same time, I felt love and pride as if I was your father, not your brother."

My dream was so real, David was still talking. I listened.

"That first picture you drew of Mom, the one she put on the refrigerator. This was your first real attempt at art and again I felt a part of your growth, because I was your first art teacher. I did feel some resentment, however, I wanted the picture to be the one I had drawn of Mom. I wanted mine on the refrigerator."

Did I say thinking about my brother makes me happy? You bet it does!

When David got older he joined the Navy.

Dear Sis:

Here I am again. I just finished writing a letter to a few people and I have come to my favorite sister. My only one. Ha. Ha. Ha.

Tomorrow I have the weekend off and am going into Oakland to see mother's cousins. They don't know it but I am going to call them up. Probably I will eat dinner there and maybe they will put me up for the night. Of course, I am not being forward. That's just life.

I am still a boiler technician and will be until July 30th. I won't be able to get a note to you because I am on temporary duty and a reserve. Do you see me worrying? No. I 'm going to write for information about various colleges. I would like to know what Buddy and Jerry are planning (oh my God he said his name out loud, Buddy, my current love). Ask Mother and Dad what they would like me to do. What do you think I should do? That's all for now except all my love. Write as you have.

Love. Love. Love.

-David

David, an artist, sculptor, writer, teacher, on the staff at the most renowned art school in Chicago. But he was always someone who was just my big brother, and, who every girl in school or anywhere, would say, "are you really David's little sister?" Hoping, of course, if they were friendly to me, then I could get him for them. And, luckily for me, he had boyfriends like Buddy who lived next door at the Sovern Hotel. Buddy, my first love, the boy I dreamt about and later saw as a man in his Army uniform, the boy I never stopped thinking about, yes, that first love.

"Anna you want to go for a walk? Maybe I'll get you some ice cream," Buddy said to me, his friend David's little sister. "Sure" I would say. Any time Buddy wanted to do something I was his and David's shadow. He parted his hair on the left side and that stayed with me. I don't like men who part their hair on the right side or God forbid in the middle. A goofy thing to like and it's my problem, I know that, but Buddy did it that way, so of course it was good.

Then one day I read in the Chicago Tribune. There it was, Section two, page eleven:

"Buddy R. beloved son of Rose and the late Tom R. died today."

Life doesn't stay the same I learned.

S.A.S.E.

CHAPTER 10

I'M MISSING MY TONSILS, MY APPENDIX, ONE KIDNEY, TWO BREASTS AND ONE EARRING WHICH I'VE BEEN LOOKING FOR SINCE LAST WEEK

It had been a year. I still felt dead. He asked me to meet him for dinner. An old acquaintance. What could I lose? I went. I had a date. I felt like a teenager. I walked into the restaurant where we had arranged to meet and I saw him. He seemed so happy to see me. He took my hand and held it and kissed me on the cheek.

It was the first time a man had touched me or had any physical contact with me since Arthur had died. I truly believed that the man was going to faint. The reason I believed he was going to pass out or throw up was because all I could think of was I'm a "breast less widow," a cancer survivor (well, not quite yet – still needed four more years). A freak, how can he even sit down and have dinner with me. I was surprised - he wanted more than dinner.

It was time to be reborn. But I was like a baby. I wasn't ready yet. A little more time perhaps. Belief in myself. Acceptance of my body and some words like "you're beautiful, I love you."

"I'll call you again," he said.

"Please do and thank you for dinner."

The next day the sun was shining, somebody, a man, loved me. My heart skipped a beat. I was excited and felt very young. I had to tell someone. My children? No. How could my children understand that I could possibly think of another man. I couldn't even believe it. You mean I might still have feelings for men, how could that be possible?

So the stirrings began and the long and painful process of birth began again and painful it was. A replay of the teenage years. The insecurities that I felt as a teenager dealing with boys were now transferred to men.

By the way, he never did call again.

*

What a long list of boys came to my door. When the doorbell rang the dog would bark. My heart would skip a beat. But "he" never came to the door they were all the PRETENDERS. The great search continued. I started looking for my husband. Sick? Yes. Determined? Yes. Successful? No. Close? Sometimes. An ear looked the same, a mannerism was familiar even eyes had the same color.

The blind date my friend and I had with the two men that never showed up. We waited four hours. These things always happen to other people. This time the other people were us. They never called, we waited and waited. Kept fixing our makeup and hair. We worried. Maybe they had an accident. By the third hour we were laughing so much about being stood up we didn't really care anymore.

The boys kept coming. The father of one of the children's friends. A widower for five years. Another dinner. I had lots of food those first few years. Well, I finally got to eat out a lot that's something Arthur never liked to do. Within the first hour after meeting this respectable older businessman, father of three children and a pillar in society, he casually mentioned that we were going to have an affair. I didn't even understand the word that's how naïve I was. I thought an affair could only be if you were married to other people. I began to learn it meant different things to different men. This little teenager was growing up.

I've heard so much about you," he said. Now, before I took a breath or thought it out, I blurted out, "I've had cancer."

"I've had a heart attack," he responded.

"I'm sorry. We certainly have a lot in common."

"What kind of cancer," he asked.

"Breast. I had a bilateral mastectomy."

"I can't deal with that. Goodbye."

He turned around and left. I turned around, leaned against the door and cried.

*

Next.

"This is it," I thought.

Our eyes met and there seemed to be an instant feeling for both of us. We met through mutual friends and he came with glowing reports from our friends. We went out for almost six months and almost immediately I knew something was wrong. I was learning.

This was an unusual blind date, because he was really good looking and sure didn't seem to need dates. He was a doctor. Very smart. But he didn't practice, he was in research at a very prestigious hospital. He even took me to see the lab he worked in and it was quite interesting. I never did know exactly why he didn't practice directly with patients anymore but he seemed happy with what he was doing.

He had five adopted kids, was divorced and didn't see his kids. They lived in another state he told me. Of course, none of that made any sense until later when I stopped seeing him. That happened when he was really acting kind of strange at times and also a bit scary.

After I gave him my official announcement "I've had a bilateral mastectomy…" he didn't seem to care and said nothing.

He was an obsessive man in many areas of his life. Also he had been involved in many physical and mental altercations with co-workers, friends and also was alienated from his original family.
His father had committed suicide a few years previously. "Shot himself in the mouth" he said in an offhand way.

One evening he interrogated me for an imaginary incident and "timed me" during a long distance phone call I received while he was visiting. I became aware of many other strange behavior patterns. Out of the blue he told me in detail about breast cancer. Facts I hadn't asked about and didn't want to know.

"I want you to look at these pictures of women who have had mastectomies."

"What?" I asked.

"They're interesting," he said.

"I don't need to see those…"

But he started to show me the pictures anyway. "Look, look!" he insisted.

I turned away and started to get away from him.

"Leave me alone," I told him.

I had overlooked these in my first feelings of caring for him. After consulting with a therapist, who he had also agreed to see, the consensus was that he was in need of help and this was suggested to him. I later found out that he was already under psychiatric care and had been for many years. Also I learned he had attempted suicide previously.

I decided to stop seeing him when it became apparent that he was unstable, possibly more than just unstable and also had become threatening to me and my children.

He told me he lived in a high rise building on the Gold Coast, Lake Shore Drive. This was an exclusive area and yes, I admit I was impressed. He did live there, but he lived in the basement apartment. He was working as a janitor because he couldn't practice medicine anymore. I was not very intuitive in those days – still in my own fog.

A year later, I learned he had jumped off the high rise building in which he had lived. He had to take the elevator up to the top to do that final act. How ironic and how sad for all who had known this intelligent, physically healthy man who had become so tormented that to him, the only peace he could find was to commit suicide.

*

Next.

I went to open the door and I thought to myself, I'm missing my tonsils, my appendix, one kidney, two breasts and one earring which I've been looking for since last week. I'm no bargain, I know. I don't know why I did it again. But as soon as Louie, Blind Date number, darn I can't even remember what number he was, walked in I told him everything. I just blurted it out. Sometimes, I even called myself a "freak" and that was very good. Then, at least they never called back.

Seeing as I was missing so many parts myself, I didn't feel I could complain. And so another man comes to my door. He was a nose picker, you know like some of the guys who do it in the car at each stoplight. It was just too much for me. Every time I turned my back, he was at it again.

Okay, one more, this is really the last. The night the guy didn't show up at all, stood up once again. Well, my face had dropped so much after waiting hours for him to arrive, that I kept freshening up for him. I had put so much powder on trying to look young, that instead, I looked exactly like Bette Davis, in "Whatever Happened to Baby Jane."

*

Next.

Ron picked me up at 6:30. It was a dinner date. Do you believe that? Not just the usual "cup of coffee" date. We sat down at the restaurant table.

He said, "I'm the chef here. I cooked a special meal for you."

"Well, thank you," I said "What a nice surprise."

The surprise was that later he also wanted more than dinner. Another man wanting more than dinner. Didn't they ever eat before they picked me up? I declined.

CHAPTER 11

MARK & SKIPPY

Back when I was still a little girl, Mark and Skippy were in my 1st grade class. We lived across the street from each other. They walked me home every day. But this day would be different. "Anna show us yours and we'll show you ours."

I didn't know what they were talking about. "If you show us, I'll show you." they said again. That sounded pretty good to me.

They showed me. The first thing I noticed was that they had something I didn't. I still to this day didn't know why they would want me to show them something I didn't have. My first experience with boys.

My first experience with a man was with the guy on the elevated train who was sitting next to me. He showed me without my asking. Just lifted the newspaper off his lap. He showed me all right.

An acquaintance of the family used to put me on his lap. A game, he called it locks. Not a good game. He wouldn't let me get off when I wanted to. He scared me, but I never knew why. I was locked, caught without being able to get off his lap. Not a game. Something felt wrong. Something was very wrong.

I grew up never quite understanding men. I was skinny, very skinny. David said "when you turn sideways, nobody can see you."

My teenage best girlfriends said to me, "you look like a stick with a head." That hurt. Teenage girls could be mean. Why, I never understood. Yet, this skinny girl was considered pretty. I never believed it, though.

My father called me "fuzzicle"– that was a bad name. I had a little bit of hair on my arms, as we all did. I was embarrassed. I was self-conscious about it and his unintentional name for me stayed with me the rest of my life. Even though I got lots of attention, I never believed it was for me, it always felt like people made a mistake and meant it for someone else, not for me. So, I bleached the two hairs on my arms my entire life. One day at age 60 I finally realized I didn't need to do that. I really am a slow learner.

*

Dear Answer Lady:

Men confuse me. I am a widow wanting to date but things have changed. Men want sex before a relationship. I grew up not knowing about the world, and always was being taken care of. How do I move on to have a real connection with someone or is that all that men want?

-Bewildered Widow

Dear Bewildered:

Men have always wanted sex before a relationship – it's time to grow up. Even if you were spoiled when you were a kid you can figure it out, you're in the driver's seat, it's your choice now to say yes or no. Good luck, dear.

-Answer Lady
(To receive a reply you must enclose a self-addressed stamped envelope.)

*

I was secure until I was eight years old. On that infamous day my father brought home a fur mouton coat, for me, not for my mother. It seemed I was the only 8 year old who had a fur coat. I hated it.

I began to have feelings that were not familiar to me. I wanted to hide so people wouldn't see me. I played a lot of hide-and-seek with my friends but I never wanted to be found. I liked the hiding part best and it was something that stayed with me until much later in life.

Then, the most embarrassing thing, worse even than the mouton coat, was the white satin, much too long dress that Dad had custom made for my grammar school graduation. I was the only one with a satin, totally very fancy, way too long, elaborate dress.

So, now, I'm really hiding, I don't want to ever be noticed again. I'm embarrassed. I'm different. I'm self-conscious. I don't want to be different and then, horror of all horrors, my mother takes me to elocution/acting lessons.

Now, I'm going to be an actress on top of all my other problems. So with all of the above going on in my little head, I have to perform in front of family and very soon after that on stage, my first role was as a grasshopper and later on I performed on radio and television. Oh my God, who am I? I became a member of the Jack and Jill Players and didn't know what a "play" was, until I was in one. My experience was therefore partly fear, partly excitement and partly "grasshopper-ish." I remember having to jump and hop around - so finally after the first feelings of fear it was now fun. I could be the child I wanted to be and even though I was supposed "to be seen and not heard" this was my chance to be both.

Amazingly enough, I was somewhat successful.

I could recite tongue twisters with great speed.

"Betty Bota bought some butter but said she that butter's bitter so she bought a bit of better butter better than that bitter butter so 'twas better Betty Bota bought that bit of better butter." The rule was no breaths just keep going.

"A big black bug bit a big black bear." Try that five times in a row.

"Peter Piper picked a peck of pickled peppers a peck of pickled peppers Peter Piper picked."

"Sister Suzy sews shirts for soldiers no one sews such soft silk shirts as sister Suzy sews."

I auditioned for commercials using material that went like this:

Most air conditioners sound like the east wind. At best they sound like — well — like air conditioners. But the new air conditioners sound like this. If we lean close, we can hear it. But our company has taken the whoosh out of air conditioners. You'll sleep better because your air conditioner is quieter.

As I aged, now pretending to be about six years old to ten:

"I don't know why it is that everybody always thinks that little girls only like to play with dolls. Every time I have a birthday or Christmas or somebody comes to visit, they give me dolls. Dolls!

Dolls are all right, I suppose. But if you play with dolls, you have to take care of them and dress them and put them to bed and everything. I don't like dolls. I wish somebody would teach me how to play baseball."

Now I am a teen: age fifteen to eighteen.

"Hello Cynthia? It's, me, Sally. Gosh, Cynth, I thought I'd never get you. I had to steal the nickels out of my mother's purse (chuckles)…that's alright…she took them out of Dad's pocket last night."

"Say, Cynthia, did he say anything? Who? He? Of course, Tommy! Is he, is he going to take me to the prom? He what? He can't get the car? Didn't you tell him I could get our car? Well, for…oops here's my Mom I'll call you back."

"Wow, an ingénue, twenty to twenty five. I never did know what an ingénue was until I was much older. But I gave it my all."

"Orchids! Mother, he sent orchids! I've never had an orchid before. And look at the size of it. I'll wear it right here…right above the sorority pin. You don't think it's too much flash do you? That's so thoughtful of him. I wonder what he looks like, but James said he's handsome. But even if he doesn't look like Alan Ladd, an orchid like this…thanks John."

Starting to think about men it seems. I wanted an orchid too and yes I did get them a few times. Some of the more sophisticated high school boys, seemed to know to buy us orchids.

I never did let the boy pin it on my dress, I just did that myself. Later on when all those things that happened to other people happened to me. I could have put pins in my fake breasts and it wouldn't have hurt a bit.

CHAPTER 12

I CAN'T SWALLOW

You have to eat they all said. Everyone kept saying you have to eat, eat, eat...

I can't swallow. I can't eat if I can't swallow. How can you eat after your husband has just been buried?

Don't tell me to eat. I have a lump in my throat. Food won't go down because it can't get through. STOP, STOP telling me to eat.

Now lunch. Lots of people. The ritual of eating so you know that you're alive. I guess that's the reason. I wasn't alive so I couldn't eat. Nobody else could either but they made the effort. It's all unreal and I'm watching it. A dream. This all must be a dream. Things are going on all around me. I am somewhere else in my head, maybe in the box with Arthur.

Tippy our lovable mutt with black and white tips on her paws, she always knew when something was wrong. She didn't eat that day either. She loved him too.

Later I would drive and have her with me when I talked to Arthur in the car. I would scream, and cry all this while driving. It was a wonderful place to release those feelings. Tippy would actually cry when I cried. We were survivors together neither one knowing what lay ahead.

I read that "time heals our wounds, time is merciful." That is partly true. I often felt a pain that was so intense that it became my evil twin. In the beginning it was always there. Even as the shock period receded the pain intensified.

I now felt as if I was in water and drowning all the time. I was depressed and anxious, scared and panicky and my long-time companion, my husband could not share it with me. It was a double loss because he was the one it was about. His comfort, our sharing the loss, was gone.

There are those who say one can commune with the dead. Maybe. Yet it's the rough touch of stubble, his beard, I missed. Arthur's hand holding mine, helping me out of the car, yes, he actually sometimes did that. His unique gravely voice comforting me when I worried.

When a young friend of ours died at an early age we shared the sadness and the loss. When any event that was a piece of our life occurred we shared that event.

So now who was there? Yes. There were a lot of people around but not the one who was my partner. After many years passed I found some kind of acceptance of Arthur's death. Finally I would remember all the times we had together. I had the memories.

I still had tears but I only cried alone. I knew nobody wanted to see me crying any more. People went back to their normal lives. It was supposed to be okay now. Well the truth be known it wasn't okay and I wasn't okay.

In the beginning, I thought about him almost every hour. The phone would ring and I was positive it was him. The doorbell - I was sure he'd come home. I'd hear the boys' voices, I thought it was him. They sounded so much like their dad. Arthur had a very distinctive voice, kind of 'raspy' and did I ever mention that he looked like John Garfield, that tough, handsome movie star? Sometimes I was even sure Arthur was in the kitchen with the kids.

In the beginning people listened to me,. They listened to every detail of what was happening to me. Now I don't even mention his name very often because I don't want memories stirred up. I desperately wanted to talk about him. As if in mentioning his name and our life he would still exist. I learned that my grief was my own private pain. It's as if he wasn't ever here.

S.A.S.E.

CHAPTER 13

HANNAH AND BEN

My mother's parents, Grandma Hannah and Grandpa Ben, owned a couple of grocery stores in Albany Park on the north side of Chicago. They arrived here in the United States from Russia by way of Canada where Grandpa Ben was promised a job and lodging but nothing worked out.

They were together for sixty years and it was from them that I learned what relationships were about. Grandma wrote her story before she died. I read it years later but I can hear her telling me that story. She's talking to me because I had a special relationship with my Grandma Hannah.

Don't tell anyone please, but sometimes I think she comes back as a bird. The one I saw so often when I sat on my screened-in porch when I was married to Arthur. The house I loved with my heart and soul.

"Two years after my mother's death, my father married my mother's sister who was a widow. My stepmother had a son in the Army. His name was Ben. His name is still Ben. My name is Mrs. Ben."

I laughed out loud. Mrs. Ben! "Grandma, Ben was your first cousin! Marrying a first cousin is not a good idea!" Grandma just smiled. I thought now there is a reason why some of us in this family are a little nuts.

Grandma just went on. "Through a lifetime together of struggle and deprivation I never had a thought of regret. There has been too much love for that."

"A year after our marriage the first of three children came to us. This was your Aunt Sonya. She was born while we were still in Russia. She was born to be blamed for everything she did wrong. And everything your mother Sarah did wrong. And everything her baby brother, your Uncle Julius did wrong.

Lucky for her Julius usually did everything right." I know that Sarah, my mother never did anything wrong. At least that's what she told me.

"By practicing the extremes of austerity we were able to amass a fortune of $200 and we used it to go into our first business venture, a grocery store. Small in size but gigantic in hours and effort. We worked from 4 a.m. to midnight every day. Then our second child, Sarah, your mother was born."

"The grocery prospered. Life became easier. We worked long hours in the store but we acquired a housekeeper. She helped raise Sonya, spoil Sarah and raise Julius who came along three years later. When Julius was born Grandpa sold the business and got a wholesale delicatessen route."

My Grandpa a truck driver? A Jewish truck driver? Another thing I never heard of.

"The next grocery store was in a prairie area in Chicago known as Albany park. We became the corned beef king and queen of Chicago together with Princess Sonya, Princess Sarah and Prince Julius. We were financially independent and pillars in the Temple. Ben was Vice President of every Shul, every synagogue/temple we belonged to. Next were grandchildren."

Here I come. Number three grandchild of six. The first girl. "And" Grandma said "for some reason or other they all liked corned beef."

Not me. I didn't follow the conventional "corned beef on rye with a dill pickle right out of a brown wood barrel and a chocolate phosphate mantra." Not me. I was a picky eater. Skinny. I still weighed under 99 lbs. until menopause, which started prematurely. Like everything else that happened too soon in my life, menopause did, too. It seemed the breast cancer surgery added that bonus, also.

Funny

My mother let me eat anything else I wanted to eat and so did most of my relatives especially Grandma. A few relatives weren't so easy on me. They made me taste things I didn't want to taste. Now another secret. I never tasted a grape or a strawberry until I was 50 years old. And another one. I buy a birthday cake, yellow with white butter cream frosting usually with pink, blue (those were my favorite colors for cashmere sweaters, also) and sometimes purple colored flowers. I'm embarrassed to say I do that, still, at least once a month. It's not my birthday, of course, I just like birthday cake. When the sales clerk asks me what name to put on it, I just make one up, sometimes, "Happy Birthday Amadeus Mozart," Betsy Ross or maybe Sophia Loren. I always try to stay anonymous so I won't be recognized the next time I come to that bakery. Okay, so I have some food fetishes, better than some other kind, I guess.

My version of loving corned beef was corned beef on white Wonder bread. Even worse it was smeared with mayonnaise and on the side tiny sweet gherkin pickles, potato chips and a couple of sips of red pop. To this day, that's still the way I eat it.

Grandma continued her story and a certain sadness sat on her heart even as her strength radiated from her. "As it is with the way of life it seems that man" and women I thought, " is not destined for an easy life." She continued.

"Tragedy struck with fury. Grandpa became very ill. He had a series of operations. His asthma – that he got when he worked in a mirror factory polishing mirrors for $6.00 a week – was always with him." Another thing my Grandpa did that I never heard of, polishing mirrors.

"In the middle of everything," Grandma continued, "Sonya's husband
died from a freak accident; had a tooth pulled, an infection developed and he died." I loved my Aunt Sonya and we had a lot in common, she was widowed early in life and struggled mightily to take care of my two cousins, and she did. However, she supported herself and the children by becoming an excellent seamstress. So, I thought to myself, *Did you hear that Dad? I told you I should have learned to sew.*

Grandma continued, "We moved to a nursing home and believe it or not, I, Hannah, who years before had been dubbed the "Queen of Corned Beef" now had another title. This time your Grandpa was included. We are King and Queen in our new home. Oh, and by the way, whenever the staff runs into a corned beef problem…"

I loved you Grandma and Grandpa.

CHAPTER 14

SCUMBAGS AND LIARS

Blind dates, oh my God, I tried. I really tried.

But I just want to tell you about the next to last guy. He had very bad breath, but that wasn't the worst of it. He also combed his hair up from the back over the top to the front, you know what I mean, don't you? He was such a nice man so finally I made it into a game. What kind of cheese would his breath smell like that night? Unfortunately it always ended up being limburger.

I stopped accepting blind dates for a long time. Instead, I became obsessed about finding another Arthur. I searched and searched.

How?

I knew I had a problem. I really wanted to get on with my life. I wanted to have a relationship but something seemed to always be in the way. I just didn't know what it is.

I met the last man, and…I'm angry. Younger or older, it doesn't matter. There are some liars and scumbags. Don't get me wrong, I like and love men. I have sons, all wonderful men, not perfect, but not liars.

I had no experience with men who lie. Now I know. His name was Max. Over and over he said "I love you" showering me with love and adoration. I loved him.

I was duped, by a liar, a man with no conscience. He fooled me. He hurt me. May be a sociopath? I don't know. All I do know was that for four years I loved him.

One day he was accidentally exposed by, of all people, the woman who cut his hair and trimmed his beard for over ten years. When my mother, who was 97 years old, met him, she told me, "he's a very nice man, he's good-looking, he seems to love you," she paused, "But don't marry him."

I was in the morning of my life and it was good. I thought it was so good that it seemed another rebirth had happened. I was in love. He was smart. He wanted to protect me. He had an accent; I loved it.

He was caring, he listened to me, and I loved him and he loved me. Why for me did it seem to always need a man to give me a rebirth? I don't know. I still don't know. Everything was beautiful. We loved each other and it was familiar to both of us. Always missing each other and each time we saw one another we felt that love.

We met at a senior center. Another well-respected widower, a very active man, did a lot of volunteer work, he said. He was a few years younger but he said, "the moment I saw you, I fell in love with you."

"I love you too" eventually, I said.

He held my hand and easily he claimed, "you're the love of my life."

"I never loved anyone the way I had loved my late wife" he said, "until you." Arthur had trouble saying the words "I love you" so it was something new to me.

But Max was different. He thought he could never love anyone again in the same way he had loved his wife. She had died more than twenty years before. Our interests were not always the same.

Max was a retired accountant. He loved numbers and the stock market so he sat at the computer every day and bought and sold stocks on margin. Somewhat risky, but he loved it. He showed me pages of all his investments, there were many pages. I didn't understand it all but my father loved the stock market, too, so it was familiar to me. I assumed he knew what he was doing. But he shared it with me, loved to talk about it and because it was important to him and he was important to me, I listened. He didn't like movies or theater much (at least not with me, I realize now) but we did go occasionally.

We ate out a lot, took walks, saw my family and some friends and just talked and talked. He did something as a volunteer that was often last minute stuff. Like taking seniors to doctor's appointments he explained. Always last minute.

I never asked much about why it was last minute. I was in love. Logic and warning pathways were turned off in my brain. I never talked about my volunteer work for the same organization, as what I did was counseling, and that was always strictly confidential so I accepted the last minute stuff easily.

The day of the discovery of who he really was and the revelation of the lies he had told during all those wonderful years we were together was now uncovered. Afterwards I remembered my mother's words and the ONLY truth from him in the almost four years was when I told him what she had said, after he had been found out, after the discovery, and he agreed that "she was right." I'm happy she isn't here to know how right she was.

One afternoon when my niece left a message for me to call her back and after I did, those almost four long years disintegrated in an instant. All my strength collapsed. I went into shock. In that instant everything changed. The shock, the disbelief, the loss was so instant and unexpected that I simply couldn't process it. It was as if I had been hit by a car. The breath was knocked out of me. Familiar, long ago feelings, of the shock of Arthur's sudden death.

I notice I gave a very long explanation for that lie of his, why am I still trying to explain him? I just didn't seem to have any reason to distrust him, and it was so many years that we had been together, I was secure with him. Where was my intuition, but why should I have been suspicious? A long sentence I now know, but what's the big deal about a long sentence? Everybody liked him. His eyes sparkled. He was sociable, we never "hid" out, but he loved to be with me only. At least most of the time. He was in "seventh heaven" he said again and again.

He scheduled our times and was always precise in just the amount of time because of the other part of his life where he might be called at anytime. We talked almost every day on the phone. I met some people in his life, but never his daughter. He always had a logical reason. My God, where was my brain! But, why would I have had any idea, we were out in the open, he was a widower, oh my God, what a fool I was. I thought he just wasn't close with his daughter and couldn't admit to it. I didn't want to keep asking him, thought it was a hurtful situation for him to admit.

I returned the call to my niece. "I need to tell you something," she said, "because I love you, because I care about you." My world collapsed. I could not believe what she told me. What's wrong with me, I thought. What did I do wrong? Why me? Oh my God, another "why me?" Why, why? Everything seemed so right.

Everybody else in my life had someone and so did I. I was very happy.

When I was hospitalized for back surgery. He came everyday, sat there, very attentive. But every so often over the years, he would have to leave suddenly to do his "volunteer work." Okay, so for all those years he said his daughter wanted to meet me, knew all about me, but things just never seemed to work out. I met his cleaning lady, I met his cronies from the senior center, however…

Did they know?

*

The only one I didn't meet was his WIFE!

They lived separately. Not true I found out, it was only when she went away for the winter it seemed. He said later, it was an "arrangement" yes, quite an arrangement, he told me after he was…

*

Caught.

"I've been going there for years to get my haircuts," my niece continued, "it wasn't close to my house, but I went there for about fifteen years. I knew her, my beautician, very well."

It was however, around the corner from where he lived, the man I loved.

And it seemed the beautician also, knew him well. So, they all knew one another very well, it seemed.

My niece described the shop, "It's very small, only two chairs, and I was in one of the chairs when I saw him walk in at the same time as another customer did. She described the woman to me; "neat looking, bleached blonde hair, very tall and heavy set."

"They sat down, and would be next after I was finished. I could see him in the mirror. When I saw him, I jumped up and ran over and kissed him on the cheek. I was very happy to see him and lovingly and kiddingly, I said, 'How's my Auntie A?' He turned pale, seemed surprised and confused, didn't answer immediately, but then said 'everyone's fine' in a not so friendly or happy voice, and definitely 'not so glad to see me' type answer. He was quite cool, so I went back and sat down to have my hairdresser complete my appointment. He started looking at the newspaper. As soon as I returned, my hairdresser frantically, but very quietly, was trying to tell me something.

"She succeeded and surreptitiously but firmly told me 'He's married, that's his wife,'" she said. "He's been coming here for about ten years."

I, of course, didn't believe a word she was telling me, she must be mistaken, I was positive. But maybe, could it be possible, the stereotype of a hairdresser was true: "she knows all, and sees all."

My niece continued telling me what her hairdresser had told her. "He lives around the corner. The wife has only been coming in every so often for a few years, but I have two other customers who know him. One told me "he played around with lots of women." One woman asked the hairdresser to tell her when he was coming in, my niece said, because she didn't want to be there when he had his appointment. She claimed he had 'groped' her!"

I hope that isn't true and I still simply cannot believe it. But who am I to know anything about anything especially about this man I loved, this man I really did love, this man who was a liar, how was I to know anything about anything, oh dear God, especially about this man I loved, really loved.

Seeing other women when we were together? He later swore that wasn't true – "it was before me" He swore! I never said anything about groping. Just couldn't get that into my brain. It was just too crazy. It couldn't be possible.

I was sure she wasn't telling the truth or the words the woman used changed over time, like the "pass the potato" game, you know, how the words change after a while after one person tells the story and then the next one tells it a little differently. Right? So he touched her arm, he was talking to her in an affectionate way, he was probably related to her? Right? He did NOT grope her, not this man I loved. Maybe the woman was a liar. She had to be. I needed to rationalize that part. I still do not believe it, this was not the man I loved. No, no, not possible, I so hoped it wasn't true.

*

Denial & Shock.

I was experiencing both. "He's a scum bag and a liar," my niece repeated, there are lots of those kinds of men. Believe it, please believe it." My niece left the shop without paying, she wanted to get out fast, but the tall woman he came in with runs out after her and says "Tell your Auntie A he's married and that she better know that so when he takes his last breath, she'll know that." The woman must have heard me ask him, "how was my Auntie A?"

Someday, I hope I meet her and tell her I didn't know he was married. I want her to know that.

Will I ever be able to trust or love again?

*

Then I saw him.

We talked. I saw him a few more times after he was found out. He called and said he had something to talk to me about. I cried. I told him how anyone I called to tell them about our relationship was happy for me. I said you were my boyfriend. I called you Honey and you called me Your Sweetheart in your native language. I introduced you that way. You were my significant other, very significant, at least to me. You met all my family and you thought they were such a wonderful and supportive family. They are, oh, yes, they really are.

I never showed my anger that day I just cried so you never got to know how angry I was. "You are an imposter, a liar, a cheat" I thought, but didn't say it. "I never thought I would fall in love again," he said after he was caught.

"I felt terrible. I didn't want to lose you." He was still saying he loved me. And I was still believing what he was saying. I was crazy. Still, I was strong enough to say goodbye on that day. At the door he said it one more time, "I still love you." And, you know what? I believed him, because if that wasn't true, the part about his loving me, it would have been impossible for me to ever, and I mean ever, to have risked loving any man again.

Did she?

CHAPTER 15

DEPRESSION

I don't feel good. I can't sleep. My body is weak, I'm sick again, I went to the emergency room and was admitted to the hospital for four days. I will need surgery for diverticulitis, I was told. I haven't got the strength right now.

I can wait awhile they said. Stress didn't cause it, but I'm sure it didn't help.

I felt like an old woman now, and yet I was hoping, waiting at the phone like a teenager. I was waiting for him to call. He did. That same day. What did stupid me think? What else? He was getting divorced. Of course, that's why he's calling.

We met, I listened, I cried. He was going to negotiate with her. "I still love you!"

Stupid me, baby me, dumb me, all that was happening to me was that I was still feeling the sadness of another loss. I couldn't get to the anger stage yet.

*

Searching.

He didn't die, although that's what it felt like for me. I can still hear him saying how he "feels so terrible. I never thought I'd ever fall in love again. I didn't want to lose you. I love you now. I'll always love you. The minute I saw you I fell in love. I never felt like this before, except for my late wife." He said this over and over again in the four years we were together. It seemed so real, that love. He said it that last day. Maybe, just maybe, he really did love me. I need to believe that part. My friends and family tell me they believe that he did love me. Thank you friends and family.

The next time I saw him was at a lecture a few weeks later and I met a friend of his who I saw and asked if she wouldn't mind talking to me for a few minutes. She had always been a little cool to me, never friendly, and I never understood it.

I assumed it was because she liked him and perhaps realized I was dating him. By the way that turned out to be the truth. She wanted to be more than his friend. I asked, "would you mind telling me what you know about your friend, something has happened and I am very confused about it."

"What's that?" she asked.

Well, I just found out that he's married.

"You didn't know?" she asked. "How could you not have known? Have you ever been to his house? Didn't you see the grand piano? Does he play the piano?" she asked me sarcastically.

I asked him. Yes, I asked him about it thinking he must have played the piano and he told me "I keep it here for a friend who has no room in her house." Another sign of this good guy who does favors for friends, he keeps a grand piano in his living room. He volunteers to bring "meals on wheels" which I now don't even know if that was true. I was proud of him; he was always helping others. He was very busy. Oh, yes, busy juggling two lives, maybe more, what do I know. There certainly didn't seem to be anyone else living there. No sign of a woman, unless she was locked up in the attic or in the basement somewhere. But why would I have had a reason to be suspicious. I met some of his neighbors, we went to lectures and events together many times. He really was a brave, no, a brazen man, taking such chances. I'm a trusting person, why would I not have trusted him? Why, someone tell me why? We looked through his old picture albums, he told me who everyone was, his late wife's picture was on the mantle. Oh, my God, how did he do it; The nerve to take me into his/her house.

So, my new woman friend, still not very friendly, continued to tell me more. I thanked her, and she left to sit down for the lecture. I did the same. A few minutes later, however, she returned to tell me, "he's here, with his wife, about 5 rows over on the right side." So she was now really my friend, I guess. Maybe she was looking for "fireworks" of some kind, or maybe, just maybe, she had had a similar experience with him?

I saw him and should have left then but I had one more piece to hopefully finish it for me. The lecture was over, he walked right past me with the woman who my niece had described perfectly; the woman in the beauty shop. I went over to him, the wife must have gone to the washroom, as he was now standing alone. "Hello" I said, "How are you?"

"I'm fine, are you okay?"

"Yes, I'm fine. Are you here with your wife?" I asked.

"Why would I be here with my wife? No, she's not here," he said with such ease.

"Really, I just saw your friend, she told me you were here with your wife."

"No, she's not here," he said again, looking me straight in the eye. "Why?" Did you want to talk to her?"

"Oh, yes, I really do," I said, "she knows my name and I want her to know that I didn't know you were married."

"It will make it harder to "negotiate" so I can leave her." Those were the words that were spoken, but he meant so he could be with me, as he had told me at the first meeting with him, after he was caught.

Those words slipped, actually, "slithered" off his tongue. It finally happened, I was through with him. Over him - truly over him.

I went to get something to take home even though there was free pizza after the lecture. I figured he was going to stay, he loved anything "free" but so do I. Don't most people? So this still doesn't make him a liar, he was still a "good" guy and paid for most of our meals together, although I often offered and he often accepted. That was okay, too.

He was generous and sometimes even bought me a gift, new pots and pans, once, a set of knives, (hope there wasn't any secret there), and other small gifts. When he was out of town one time, with his daughter and her husband, he said he couldn't remember my phone number and so later on, he had her put it in his cell phone.

Another lie, of course. His daughter knew nothing about me so he might have asked her to do so but not telling her the truth as to who I was. I don't know anything. I am a person with no solid brain for liars. I never have been. I wonder though, will I ever be able to trust again?

He seems to like small unisex beauty salons, and small out of the way restaurants. He was obviously a brave man, thinking he was beyond getting caught, told me once, he had a lot of tickets for parking in the city. He actually seemed proud of this fact, and of course, I asked, "why don't you just pay them, do the right thing, so you won't be afraid to drive in the city?"

His excuse was lame and I didn't accept the answer and argued why he should pay for what he did wrong. I didn't like it, and hoped that wasn't the entire man I knew. It was at the beginning of our relationship and at times I would bring it up and he seemed to ignore it or just change the subject. It was a piece that was uncomfortable for me and I put it out of my mind, mostly, but wasn't able to convince him otherwise. I loved him, I rationalized that "nobody's perfect," but, obviously, I didn't know this man very well, yet, and all the "good" things about him seemed much more than this "bad" piece.

So I go get my carryout and turn around and see him and his wife sitting two feet away from me and eating. Her back is to me, he sees me and continues his meal, as if I was invisible. My only satisfaction that day was he didn't get his free pizza; he left the lecture immediately and must have told his wife he didn't feel like eating pizza.

*

Anger.

Now, finally, I'm really angry. Yeah, finally. Our politics are quite different. That's okay. He had a big political sign stuck on his lawn. He often said I was a "lefty liberal." I didn't care. I am an independent political thinker, but I don't literally wear a political hat insulting people that don't agree with me or put derogative labels on people. He did. I was in love. I was stupid.

On that last day, he explained to me about his wife. "She was very persistent, wanted to get married, had never been married before, and she had helped him out with his child when his wife died so he helped her out and married her? I was in love, I was stupid.

Maybe, just maybe, there was some money there? Now, that's a good guy, right? married someone to be a good guy. He thought he would never fall in love again (until he met me, he said) and she was a determined woman. I was in love. Still stupid.

I wish I knew how I could have been so dumb; it's very hard for me to think I missed so many clues. But, if he loved me, and at the time it seemed true, and, yes, I loved him-the man I thought he was.

And it was good when I thought he was honest and free.

But, as he walked out of the door those childhood words came to me, "liar, liar, pants on fire!"

CHAPTER 16

SATURDAYS

I remember the Saturdays when my brother-in-law would come over on his way home from work. I would make lunch, usually leftovers from Friday night dinner, chicken soup with rice or noodles, sometimes, matzo balls from the recipe on the Manischewitz box and chicken sandwiches. I would serve at least eight to ten people for lunch. There was always somebody I would be making a chicken sandwich for. If I didn't have enough chicken I would improvise with peanut butter and jelly or lettuce and tomato sandwiches.

Lucky for them, but not so for Arthur when one of his first meals that I cooked for him was "boiled" (no, I didn't forget to put the 'r' in as in 'broiled'). I knew nothing about cooking in those early days so I boiled those very expensive lamb chops. Ugh.

Those days seemed so hard at the time and now as I think back it's a fond memory. I miss it. It was togetherness. It was family. Everybody would come to our home on Saturday, the neighbors, the children's friends and a bachelor friend would stop by every Saturday. There was always somebody there and we would just sit around and talk. No television, just talk. I wonder why sometimes I didn't like it. I felt put upon I guess, as if I was holding it all together. I wasn't and yet I felt I was in some way. Something about the food; what to eat. Later when my daughter and I were alone we hardly ever ate together. We just had a meal here and there, most of the time we just didn't make anything out of it. I don't feel much like a family anymore, I feel fragmented. In retrospect, I do miss it. It was good, it was real, it was my family.

Our dog barked at everybody who would walk in; constant tumult, very lively. I remember a friend saying, "How can you stand all the noise and excitement?" and I remember telling her, "I like it." Now I know why; it was alive, it was life.

These days I'm so tired of struggling with money problems and so sometimes small things bother me; when kids call their parents by their first names, feeling responsible for everyone's happiness. It's hard to believe that I can't be everything to everybody.

But, babies and young children make me smile.

I'm a survivor. I learned that survivors are people with hope. I learned that survivors, after experiencing trauma or loss often feel reborn. I was reborn.

In my line of work, I am often helping those struggling with cancer to reduce their stress, this makes me feel good. I'm a helper. I try to help people with what they want, not what I think they want.

"Be kind, for everyone you meet is fighting a battle." Thank you, Plato.

"Want what you have." Thank you, Confucius.

"Live with an attitude of gratitude."

Yet here I am thinking about those years of loss and being reborn – a collage of memories like breastfeeding my daughter Judy behind a closed bedroom door. It's quiet with the warmth of the sun shining through the window giving sustenance to another human being and feeling safe.

I had tried before with my boys but now I was determined to succeed and I did, capturing an intimacy I had never experienced before. Now even with a double mastectomy I still feel the joy long ago of that experience.

My daughter Judy grew up, moved to a new life and new country. She is a totally independent woman. She works hard and is always learning new things. She recently was trained to be a doula – assisting other women during labor to give birth in a more relaxed way. It brings back a memory of when she was born. I hope she knows how lucky I am to have her. The day I was being discharged from the hospital the nurse brought her in wrapped up in a blanket with the new bonnet on her dark, full of curls, head of hair. I was ready to leave, I looked at her and because her hair was covered she looked different that day. I decided to change her diaper before Arthur came to take us home. I unwrapped her blanket, took off the old, wet diaper and luckily, I didn't faint.

My baby girl had a teeny, tiny, penis!

Yep, the nurse brought the wrong baby to me, and if I hadn't had a girl, after three boys, I might have never known there had been a terrible mistake.

She is strong, bright, beautiful and genuine. She and my son-in-law together raise their five very special children.

Judy had written a note to give her Daddy and was so excited to be able to see him again after the five days he had been hospitalized. She never did. She was nine when he died.

My oldest son, Bill, went to live in California after he married. He suffered with asthma growing up and had a difficult childhood because of it. Yet, as the oldest child, he felt a responsibility for his brothers, sister and me. One day he called to say "Mom, I'm moving back to take care of you." I said "no, I'm getting stronger you don't have to do that."

This was the same, now grown up son, who at four years old said, "My friend asked me to be president of a club, Mom, can I? "Sure, you can," I said. He then asked "What's a club?" Later he became Senior Vice President of a division of a worldwide company, quite a bit larger sort of club.

He's a respected, successful business man, sought after as a consultant and has been a mentor to many. An avid reader, very intelligent, loves music as his father did. He is a devoted father to his two wonderful boys and yet, he is still always there for me and others.

My second son, Ron, is sensitive to others needs and can't say no to anything anybody asks of him. As a young boy he used to pick flowers for a little girl he loved on our block. When a neighbor told him he couldn't pick the flowers in the cul-de-sac, three year old Ron cried. Drying his tears he instead 'drew' a picture of the flower he had wanted to give her.

As a talented musician he continues his creativity and sensitivity with great love and is deeply invested in others lives. He loves animals and is very philanthropic.

He was the entrepreneur always starting a business; fixing all the neighbors kids bikes, delivering papers, and then fixing up and using our crawl space as he and big brother Bill, as his senior partner, collected photos of girls from magazines and charged money for other kids to see them! When Arthur and I finally discovered why so many kids were coming in and out of our front door…all we could think of was that it was obviously a sign of their future business successes, and quite an embarrassment to their parents, us.

When I had Marty the doctors wouldn't let me see him for seven days. Seven days not seeing my third boy. He was premature and the hospital kept him in one location in the hospital and me in another section. The hospital was undergoing construction and they wouldn't take the incubator to my bedside and wouldn't let me go to him. Arthur rented a Polaroid camera to prove to me that he was okay. He took pictures of our new baby but they were so dark and blurry, I still couldn't believe that even Arthur wouldn't tell me the truth. I think he thought the camera was broken. Poor new Daddy, Arthur trying his best to stop my fears. But I needed to see my baby, needed to count his fingers and toes.

Well, he was a perfect baby. Now a wonderful man, extremely intelligent. Always still learning and helping others. He works as a consultant for schools and therapists. Had a short paper published in the Journal of his profession. He is respected and admired in his field of work. He works with people with special needs. AND he still has perfect fingers and toes! AND (he wouldn't let me say anymore great special fabulous things about him.)

When the children were growing up we used to have family meetings once a week. We called it the "family club" or "Chai" which means life. All six of us met on our queen-size bed and the meetings were often noisy, wild, lots of wrestling, hitting, laughing, and crying, but it was a way to try to keep peace between the kids. It gave them their chance to ask for something or suggest ideas and we would consider and listen to them. Arthur, was always the president, however, as he explained, we were not a 'democracy' but a 'benevolent dictatorship' and as President, he was in charge. What's a 'bevol' someone dared to ask. And Arthur, their Daddy, explained. "I pay the bills, I feed you and I make the rules. But, I will do it in a kind, considerate, friendly, good, way. You just have to mind your Mother and me." He would call the meeting to order with the usual greeting, "Now, would you all quiet down."

I was the secretary and would read the minutes of the previous meeting: "Dog poop is still in the back yard. Each of you had a day to clean it up." A fine was levied against the three boys on the bed." We will collect a penny from each of you at the end of the meeting." Judy never had to pay because she didn't get an allowance, she was too little. This did not sit well with her brother, Marty, who was closest in age and seemed to still like the position of 'baby' if he could get away with it.

Crying and shouting and whining erupts "I forgot" "I'll do it now" "I didn't see it but I got some on my shoes" "I couldn't find the pooper scooper." Judy is jumping up and down on the bed and Marty pushes her down. She screams. "I didn't hurt her she is such a baby," he says.

Fines are levied again and again. The president announces that the secretary i.e. me, is now in charge. Meeting is adjourned. I say over the unruly group wrestling with each other, "out of here now – go do your jobs" and soon the commotion passes just like life.

CHAPTER 17

LARRY, PRETEND HUSBAND

I worked full time under the supervision of psychologists at my local hospital. Later when I no longer had little kids with me and Arthur was long gone, I facilitated therapy sessions for patients in the psych units. I also gave neuropsychological tests, memory tests, I.Q. and many other kinds of tests to patients who had traumatic brain damage. Those who had suffered a stroke, got tested to see if there was any damage and then how to help in the recovery process. The patients were young and old with many different diagnoses and later I did volunteer and private client work particularly for cancer patients. I studied and worked as a biofeedback therapist, taught relaxation strategies and later was certified as a stress management educator. I met all kinds of people and, sure, I should have known better, when I met Larry.

*

It was many years since Max was out of my life. I was lonely for the ordinary conversation with a man. Having someone look at me with love in their eyes. Then I met Larry. I was ready and able to feel love again and so was he. We fell in love. We decided to marry. It had been 15 years and I was ready. Well, I thought I had married in a ceremony surrounded by family and friends. But he said he forgot to bring the marriage license and our marriage was therefore a sham. If I were making notes for a client file they would look something like this:

> Fits the psychological definition of borderline personality.
>
> Boy physically abandoned by father. Mother emotionally abandoned him. Now client has personality (character) disorder. Sometimes called borderline or paranoid. Client denies being sad. Transfers energy that might be used to feel and express emotions into more repression. Says "that's the way I am." This ingrained in character. Experiences feelings as frightening. He doesn't allow emotion to surface. Often says: "I just leave and never look back."
>
> Does not appear to have any genuine feelings. Affect appears normal and yet he seems out of touch with basic emotions. Emotionally immature and self centered. Intimacy and caring are lacking. Rationalizes his behavior. He breaks agreements, is extremely untrustworthy, often disappearing or just not showing up.

Holds on to anger, bears grudges, easily slighted. Reacts suddenly and unpredictably with anger. Metes out punishments to others by not speaking to them. He says, "I am nothing, nobody has ever heard me or listened to me. I'm a failure. I'm a nothing - you're a nothing." Orchestrates situations to prove he is unworthy.

Limited control and he literally runs away as parents did. Says in his little boy voice, "I always told you, it's not too easy, life is hard." Frantic efforts to avoid real or imagined abandonment. Low self-image. Unstable. Many relationships with women. This is a good hearted boy in a man's body." End of client notes.

He wasn't my client he was my "pretend" husband and when I first met him, he charmed me immediately.

Larry was a very handsome man. I loved to look at him and I did that a lot. He was a good listener and women were openly attracted to him and openly flirtatious.

Many years later, the chapter on "mental disorders" right out of the (DSM) the Diagnostic Criteria Coding System was perfect. His personality character disorder was right on track. Lucky for me we never did get that Illinois State marriage license in time for our pretend wedding ceremony. But three days before the "wedding" I got the kidney cancer shocking news. Now more cancer. My bout with bronchitis and an x-ray taken caught part of my kidney. And two days later I had surgery to have it removed, a new word, nephrectomy, now added to my vocabulary. This time it was only a kidney, but I didn't feel as if I lost my femininity, it didn't make me feel like a "freak." He did stay with me, in my tiny studio apartment, while I tried to be brave as I recovered, and still be a "new bride" until we were able to move. It wasn't easy for him and he did get slightly irritable at times as I hurt a lot and did do a lot of "moaning." But I did like having someone say "I love you" even though it wasn't quite as often as when I still had that left kidney.

By the way, he did have many good qualities, just very difficult to live with the bad kind. Like when we would walk into a restaurant and the hostess would ask "how many?" I would answer," two" then walk to our table and assume he would be following; however, he would have disappeared. Honestly, he was gone. Just disappeared without a word.

Larry even left me at an airport once and he had our tickets. I waited and waited and stayed exactly where he left me sitting until there were only about five minutes left. I ran to the gate and there he was hiding, yes, actually hiding behind a pillar in the corner of the waiting room. I saw him. I asked him for my ticket, he gave it to me and I boarded the plane.

He followed me on board. Saying it was my fault. I scared him. Why? Because I had asked him "do you know if the plane is on time?" and he thought that was criticism. So, when he came out of hiding, he walked on to the plane, sat down next to me without a word. We had a very quiet trip home.

It turned out that Larry had married three women before me. When I asked him one time, "how come you never married again after your divorce?"

"I did," he answered.

Oh, but you told me...

Larry interrupted me, "I thought it might scare you off," he said. Another man who was afraid the truth would scare me off.

So, who was she, do I know her, what's her name?

"Rose, Babs, Maureen and Sharon"

Oh my God! You were married four times?!?

So, I say it again. Thank God, he was just a "pretend" husband."

I didn't know that either. I really was lucky that the license didn't arrive in time.

So, I certainly know I'm not perfect, far from it, but it sure does seem since Arthur, I don't have great taste in men.

CHAPTER 18

ISRAEL: THE NO FLY ZONE

Dear Answer Lady:

I'm ready to move on with my life and travel alone to see my grandchildren. It's sad they don't have any Grandpa but they have me and I am determined to see them even though some of them live 7000 miles away from me. Help.

-Afraid to Fly

Dear Afraid to Fly:

Stand up straight and move on. You can and will find a way. Get some help from a travel agent. There are ways to travel these days that might work for you. Good Luck.

-Answer Lady
(To receive a reply you must enclose a self-addressed stamped envelope)

*

I miss my grandchildren so much that at times it feels as if my heart is broken in half. My tears at those times could fill the oceans or the miles that separate us.

I don't feel or get angry very often. I usually get sad. The sadness I felt when two of my children moved to another country was unbelievably painful. When I knew I couldn't change the situation, I realized how powerless and angry I really was.

There came a time when I said to myself and to them living in Israel so far away: "I'm so lonesome, I need to come to see you even though I don't fly anymore. I'm looking for a way."

The decision not to fly came after many years of suffering extreme ear pain on every flight. I saw numerous doctors and even called NASA asking: "how do the astronauts handle ear pressure pain? I am willing to put on a space suit and a helmet. I'll sit in the back of the plane". I didn't care how foolish I looked, just wanted to visit my kids at least one time a year.

"No luck," said NASA, "no such thing for civilians." The gratifying part of speaking to NASA was that they understood the extent of my ear pain and that I wasn't imagining or magnifying it. I had validation that I wasn't a wimp, or just afraid of flying.

The thought of bursting an eardrum hundreds of feet up in the air was a real possibility and that did not appeal to me. Just couldn't get my Eustachian tubes to adjust to the change in air pressure. Finally surgical implantation of tubes was successful. But, with the prospect of scar tissue developing after doing this many times I decided not to repeat the surgery and never fly again without the ear tubes.

Yet the prospect of never seeing my children and grandchildren who lived in Jerusalem, Israel, loomed large and no longer seemed possible. My California son, daughter-in-law and two grandsons, that was possible. My Chicago son and daughter-in-law, that was very easy to do. I loved seeing them and they stayed, as my "hostages" in Chicago.

My son who lived in Israel and my daughter, son-in-law and five other grandchildren was a different story. There must be a way to get to Israel without taking a plane I thought. Having gone through many challenges that became problems to solve this seemed like just one more thing to figure out. I remembered how Dostoevsky said "taking a new step, uttering a new word, is what people fear most." I would be more afraid of not taking a new step. "No that can't be done" said the travel agent when I asked how to get to Israel without flying. Then one after another the phone calls came.

"There is no way," all the travel agents told me.

"Anna, it can't be done" said my friends shaking their heads.

I researched on my own. Then I found a young, enthusiastic travel agent who followed through with some information. She had used the Euro rail train system and thought it might be possible. It would be a different type of trip than she was used to booking, very long and arduous. No doubt as she looked at this senior citizen would-be-traveler she must have thought to herself; there are youth hostels but are there any "old-people hostels?"

The dream began to really take shape in reality.

Money was one deterrent. I decided I would use some of my retirement funds while I was not so old, despite what the travel agent thought, was healthy and could still walk. I would take time off from my full time job, use the benefits I had accumulated for vacations and now I was ready.

I was persistent and learned that when an agent used the words "they would try" often meant they would lie and that "they could do it" was the real answer. This has become my philosophy of life. Not always easy but worth the effort.

I discovered there were freighters that took passengers across the ocean. They were unable to give a timetable as to how long it would take to cross the Atlantic Ocean. It could take many months I was told and the cost would reflect that fact and it could be extremely expensive. That left the only other way to get across the Atlantic, the Queen Elizabeth the Second (the QE2). The legendary and out of the realm of possibility luxury ship. "I can't afford this," I thought when I discovered the QE2. Then I had a second thought, there must be a way.

I wrote to QE2 Cunard Ship Line Personnel Department in England. "Can I work my way across the ocean teaching Stress Management and Relaxation Techniques?" This was my profession (not that people who can afford to take a vacation like that don't have stress, but they are able to afford travel on the QE2 so are already feeling more relaxed.) I was clutching at straws now. Yet, still I persisted, I would not give up.

One very helpful representative of Cunard Lines told me there was something called matched sailing dates, you leave on one date and must return on another particular date. The cost is 50% off the original price. Okay, now we're on to something. Of course, I had already been told no employment positions were open, but they would keep me in mind for future sailings. I contacted the travel agent and my dream was now becoming a reality.

Day One: Friday, August 19

I went to Chicago's Amtrak Union station. It has been beautifully restored to its original beauty and I peeked into the VIP lounge to leave for New York. I decided someday I would go in there. Passengers are treated very differently at Amtrak when you're taking a sleeper which I was not. Years later I did that too. The train ride was one of the bumpiest rides I had on the entire trip. During the night it felt like a bucking bronco. But I hadn't been on the train through Italy yet.

Day Two: Saturday, August 20

At breakfast in the train's dining car I was seated with three other people. A young Asian girl, about 20 years old, sat next to me. On Amtrak the stewards seat you and they must have four to each table, no exceptions. My seatmate hardly spoke any English, and she seemed unable to order her breakfast. I helped her to do so by describing the choices using hand language and silly expressions on my face.

As she was drinking her coffee she picked up a pat of butter and was about to put it in her coffee. I stopped her shaking my head no and she looked so embarrassed, I felt sorry for her. What would lie ahead for me on this trip?

The QE2.

We entered the terminal where the ship was docked and were greeted by a gentleman in a black tuxedo playing lovely classical music on a violin. I was so excited that I hardly heard it. I just knew something sounded wonderful. This was just the beginning.

The ship departed four hours after boarding and I was one of the passengers standing on the deck of this huge vessel and watched New York disappear on a beautiful, sunny August day. Seeing the Statue of Liberty from this enormous ship was awe-inspiring. I thought of how it must have looked to my father when he arrived, all alone, not on the QE2, but on the Kaiser Wilhelm, an Austrian ship, when he was a very young boy.

Day Three: Sunday, August 21

I explored this huge hotel called the QE2. I was treated like royalty. The stewards took my luggage and I never touched it after that. They were courteous, offering to help me every time I turned around. This time I felt like royalty much more so than on the train from Chicago to New York. I found I had no problems being alone.

I remembered something I had read and written in a journal after I ended my relationship with Max. "Being independent often makes me feel unsafe. Being independent makes me feel lonely. Being independent makes me feel strong and happy." It was the last part of that entry that was true now.

At meals I was seated with two other single women from England, a couple from Florida, a young man from New Jersey with his Jersey accent and another English couple.

The English people were almost impossible to understand due to their thick English accents. I felt as if I was with Monty Python. I'm certain they didn't understand me any better with my Midwestern twang.

Day Four: Monday, August 22

We were advised a mandatory life jacket drill was to take place at 10 a.m. My emergency station was situated directly in front of the roulette table in the casino. "Oh-oh," I thought, "this could be more dangerous than the ship having problems." No one knows I'm a secret gambler. I have little money to practice my vice but I never would have put myself in such a tempting position right in front of my favorite pastime: the roulette table.

Then there are the "gentlemen hosts." Another new experience. They are aboard to make sure we single women have someone attending to them. It was fun to be asked to dance over and over. Some of the rules for these hired hosts must be to avoid all eye contact and not to get involved with any of the guests. It was like dancing with robots.

This same day we had been warned of a hurricane called "Chris" which was predicted to affect us. Very scary. We had changed our course, so the impact was milder, but still bad. This was my first hurricane experience.

Day Five: Tuesday, August 23

The Captain's Greeting in the Queens dining room was a cocktail party. I went to it and had my picture taken with the Captain. Then my courage left me and I snuck out as soon as possible. I couldn't find anybody I knew and felt my usual cocktail party self-consciousness.

Later, that evening, I danced with the Cruise Director, Peter, who must have also had orders to dance with the older or single ladies. I danced again with all the gentlemen hosts.

If you like to dance then you will be happy on a cruise. It is, however, weird having such close body contact with complete strangers. Kind-of like being in the movie theater and seeing a very explicit feature sitting next to someone you've never seen in your life.

Day Six: Wednesday, August 24

I attended a grandparent's get-together where we shared grandchildren stories and pictures. I won the prize for having the youngest grandchild. I won a stuffed lion wearing a Cunard Company Line sweater. The grandparents' activity also gave me the chance to practice pronouncing my Israeli grandkids names. Not easy when you don't speak Hebrew.

Day Seven: Thursday, August 25

I couldn't believe this was the last full day on the ship. It went so quickly. I had experienced so much, dining with people from other countries, watching the ocean slide by, sitting on the deck chairs and wondering how others had traveled this route before me. I had matured, gained courage to try new foods and was very proud of myself.

I tweezed my eyebrows by the light of the porthole. I was fortunate to have a porthole because for the half-price rate I was supposed to share a cabin and have an inside room with no porthole. I got lucky and my accommodations were left the same even though the unknown woman, by the name of Evelyn, never appeared. I waited every night for her to show up because there was even a bottle of champagne in the cabin when I first arrived, for Evelyn, not for me. Oh well, I think she must have missed the boat – literally and figuratively. It was a bonus having my own room.

Day Eight: Friday, August 26

South Hampton, England. After five elegant, pampered days on the ship I found that I was really unable to drag, pull or lift my suitcases. I tried to pack very lightly, and thought I had done so, but something needed to be done. Now I knew some things had to be eliminated from my luggage or I couldn't move or continue my trip.

I unloaded and give up precious items (the converter which meant no hair drier usage or the use of the hair curling iron) - already I looked and felt different. I just couldn't give up the large paperback book I was reading (thank you sister-in-law, for this next bit of advice you gave me once.) I tore off half of the book that I had already read and with terrible guilt, about tearing up a book, I did it anyway. That lightened my load somewhat.

What became important were safety pins, plastic baggies and thank goodness, crackers. Cute outfits were given up quickly. In my haste to unpack, I later found that I had put only one shoe in the giveaway box, so the one remaining shoe in my carry-on suitcase was of no use. I found a way to a post office and sat on the floor and eliminated all those things. I was shocked when they told me it would cost $200 dollars to send that box to Jerusalem.

It seemed the only way and the nice people at the South Hampton post office suggested addressing it to the Jerusalem Main Post Office because I couldn't find the kid's addresses. I never thought I'd see any of it again but about five days later it actually arrived and we went to pick it up.

Now, the first ferry and on to Cherbourg, France. This was an overnight trip but no food was included.

Day Nine: Saturday, August 27

I had no time to eat because I had to catch a train, so I ate my meal on a sparkling clean train to Paris. What a meal, crumbled, shmooshed cracker crumbs.

Day Ten: Sunday, August 28

"Oh my God" I'm in Paris. Six hours with Leonardo, the taxi driver whom I convinced to show me Paris in the six hours I had before I was onto the next destination. And "did he ever show me," as they said back in those days, "Paree." The Musee de Orsy, the Left Bank, the Eiffel Tower, Montmartre; I was dazzled by it all.

I departed France via a train and arrived at the next train station. I then had to change trains to go to Brindisi, Italy. This was my first real nightmare. I couldn't get up the train steps and could not find anyone to help me. I finally struggled up the steps and then could not get through the aisles because they were jam packed. There were people literally on top of people. Somehow I made it.

I found my couchette mates, Eric from Germany, Peter from Italy, Isabel from France, a no-name lady, about 85 years old, carrying her own bag. Oh the shame of my weakness struggling with my bags as she easily handled hers.

The couchette was made to sleep six people and it was only the size of a very small closet. The couchette mates were coughing, sneezing, and talking all night. My bunk was on the top. During the night, I needed to use the bathroom. I climbed out of my bunk and opened the door walking down the corridor to the bathroom. It was just a hole in the floor. Then coming back into the pitch-dark couchette this very scary guy tapped me on the shoulder as I returned. I screamed, waking up all my couchette mates and this started all the sneezing and coughing up again. Yin yang torture, but worth it because this ride had the most gorgeous scenery, the bluest of blue water and magnificent seaside resorts along the way.

Day Eleven: Monday, August 29

I arrived in Brindisi, Italy, and had the first real meal since getting off the QE2 at a small restaurant near the dock. Nothing looked familiar – but there was bread and pasta and that I knew something about.

Day Twelve: Tuesday, August 30

By now, I was awfully glad I kept the hand wipes when I made choices of what to keep and what to send on to Israel. The water was just a trickle in the bathrooms of some of the trains and ferries and often didn't even have a trickle left in it and toilet paper – no such thing.

On this next ferry from Italy to Greece, I once opened a door that had no warning sign on it and it went straight into the sea. Poseidon and me fast friends at last. I would have gone there had not a scruffy, tough looking sailor, in a dirty white uniform not grabbed my hand and wagged his finger "no" at me.

Days Thirteen - Fifteen: Wednesday, August 31- Friday, September 2

I arrived in Greece and couldn't make connections for three days so I was able to explore Greece. I saw the Acropolis, Parthenon, Delphi, Corinth, and these were just some of the extraordinary highlights of Greece. I finagled a very elderly man (older than even me) who passed by with a horse and buggy to take me up to the Parthenon because there was no available transportation at that time.

This was quite a harrowing ride amid the Athens auto traffic. His horse and buggy was no match for all the autos. But what fun to be riding this way in the streets of Athens. Again I felt a little like royalty with the horses clip clopping as we rolled along.

Day Sixteen: Saturday, September 3

The next ferry was an adventure a bit like the movie Gaslight with Ingrid Bergman and Charles Boyer. I was on the last leg of my journey. I couldn't believe I was on my way to Haifa, Israel. This was an overnight trip and as the ferry pulled away from the dock there we were in the Ionian Sea going toward Greece. The Mediterranean water was as blue as I had seen in photographs. I was almost there. As the wind blew my hair off my face I thought about all those who had gone before me on this water. It seemed I floated along on history. We made port at the Greek Island of Rhodes and passengers departed and more came aboard.

I asked a rough looking sailor wearing a cap with the ferry logo on it about Rhodes. He shrugged and walked away. Maybe he didn't know English but he also didn't care to have a conversation. I know for a fact the crew was determined to drive the passengers crazy. They would ignore us, not answer any questions, gave no safety instructions and actually wouldn't even tell us when we could eat. It seems food has been an important part of my life, but everybody wanted to eat before the two day trip was over, so it wasn't just my old habits creeping in. Or, then again, maybe it still goes back to when the depression hit and Mom lost her milk and I was deprived of my food.

Towels were a precious commodity. I finally gave up asking for one and instead used the sheet off my bed. We arrived one full day late, actually had only one engine still working and our very mean crew. This company went out of business a few days after we arrived which seemed just right. On the way back I was supposed to take it back but it was no more. The return trip was much smoother.

The ferry arrived in Haifa, a magnificent sight and a very exciting, lively port city. There on the dock were my children and grandchildren. Immediately the joy of seeing them erased all the negative aspects of this last ferry. This was the thrill of all thrills. My heartache disappeared instantly. The pain of my children living so far away was now replaced by the joy of touching, hugging and seeing them in person.

Finally, Israel.

I woke up each morning to a picture of Arthur with our daughter at about three years of age sitting on his lap. This picture and another one that I had given her had been hanging in our home when the children were very young and so for me, it was déjà vu every day. That morning in Israel I wrote my first poem:

My Screened-In Porch

The screens are torn from tiny hands, pushing through them,
Trying to go out, trying to come in.
Just outside, lush, green fern surrounds large red flowers,
Their name escapes me now.

The air is still;
The tiny hands are quiet, taking a nap.
I close my eyes,
I wait for the breeze to come through the screened-in-porch.

The floor is cool, painted blue now.
Underneath, many different colors, so many feet have worn it out.
Once, just a cement floor, now, it has a life of its own,
With the bright sky blue it boasts as its cover.

I look up. The thrill still exists. I experience the skylight.
The thought is always there, "it's up so high, how will I clean it?"

I never did. The rain, the snow, the wind, they did it for me.

It's getting late now. The sun is setting.
I hear the baby waking from her nap.
The boys will be home from school soon. Back to the inside now.
The lovely solitude of my screened-in-porch
Will have to wait for another time.

My memories of our screened porch disappeared quickly. The intense desert heat was almost and often unbearable for this Chicago born and bred senior citizen. Feeling faint daily from the heat, walking on the stones of the unpaved streets where my children live gave me the feeling of being a pioneer again. I was really taken back in time to being a young mother and wife when Arthur and I lived in an undeveloped area that was just being developed near Chicago.

It was quite a feat to be able to take care of three children all still in diapers. Now my daughter was happily and beautifully doing the same thing. But oh, the diapers, the diapers. The two older babies were adjusting to the newest baby with the "terrible-twos" stage of development emerging at times.

The view of the hills of Judea, so different from Chicago's flat land, was magnificent. The twisting, winding tortuous mountain road we drove on every day and every dark night, was frightening for me. My son's sparse living arrangements made sharing space with him impossible even though it was cooler there. I walked more than I ever had in all the years of my life. This changed me forever. I used to be the one who would drive around and around until I found a parking space right in front of my destination. Not any more. Now I walk because I enjoy it. I took to carrying a tiny purse and find no need for my heavy one anymore. Another burden lifted.

I spent a never-to-be-forgotten cherished day alone with my oldest granddaughter. We went to a park and took a long, long walk. She, of course, needed to go to the bathroom as soon as we arrived when we were in an area where there didn't seem to be any facilities so I finally gave up and told her she could go behind a bush and I would keep her hidden. This was something she said she often did so I didn't feel guilty. However, I was surprised to find out that she wasn't the only one doing this behind that same bush at the same time.

The rain, lightning and thunder in the desert, so awe inspiring, so different from home.

The holiday of Simchat Torah; celebrating the finishing of the complete reading of the Torah and then the starting over again at the beginning.

The dichotomy of the men dancing, carrying their babies on their shoulders, and holding the Torah but also carrying guns in their belts to protect themselves and their families.

The Mediterranean Sea; the warmth of the sea and the sun in Gush Katif, a beautiful resort area in the Gaza Strip. The begonias outside the door of our room at the resort and the memories this evoked for me. The sight of my son in the synagogue looking so much like his father. The ride to the resort passing through enemy territory and the sight of soldiers, from both sides, looking like little boys with rifles slung around their shoulders.

The granddaughter's first boyfriend at the restaurant (a three-year old boy who took a liking to her) and he wanted to pet her leg. She liked it!

The two-year old dancing alone in the courtyard at the resort for over an hour dressed only in her diaper and oblivious to all around her - what a sight.

The newest infant beginning to be a responsive, adorable baby.

We're starting to bond.

Now it's time to leave Israel, to say my goodbyes. My tears flowed, I just can't control that, my 'leaky eyes,' I call it. I found I was alone, once again. I had retrieved my life with my kids and now I was to readjust once more. I said goodbye to my daughter, my son-in- law and my grandchildren. Now, it was only my son and I who drove the three hours it took to get back to Haifa for the last goodbye.

The old familiar heartache was beginning to come back.

I will never forget any of this remarkable adventure. The contrasts, the creativity needed to survive this trip, the wondrous, magnificent scenery, almost indescribable, the Greek Isles, Italy, Lake Como, the train passing through Switzerland (when I saw a McDonald's truck on a highway and I thought I was hallucinating), the autumn change of colors, the Swiss Alps, the huge imposing poplar trees, waterfalls, the beauty of it all. Most of all, my children, oh, yes, my children.

Riding four trains in one day. The time when I had only five minutes to change from one train to the next and the next time when I was given the bonus of one extra minute for another change. Eating crackers and drinking and finding bottled water everywhere. Memories come flooding back in my dreams now. I dream about drachmas, francs, pounds, lire, shekels, ships, trains, beautiful sights and sounds, but most of all, I remember the extraordinary, gorgeous, handsome, loving faces of my children and grandchildren.

And I did it all – from here to there – without flying.

CHAPTER 19

MOTHER

Now I'm back home from my trip to Israel. Every day I think about my grandchildren and children. I email them. We call each other. Believe it or not in my loneliness sometimes, I even want my mother. Yes, I want my mother. You see, I'm an orphan now. An old orphan.

Mom talked about getting ready to die, a lot. I couldn't. I wouldn't. David did. I suppose there was a piece of my father in me, I sometimes used denial to get through things and I knew I might regret it but something held me back. I waited too long, she went back to the hospital a few days later, didn't feel good. David and I spent the day with her and went home quite late.

The nurse called almost as soon as I got into bed to go to sleep. I should come right over she told me, Mom's asking for David and me. I said, please tell her I'll be right there. It was 11:30 p.m. I got dressed and rushed to the car.

I arrived about 25 minutes later. I went right into her room. The nurse told me I could.

She forgot to tell me she was already dead.

She also forgot to close her eyes. I saw my mother, still with her eyes open. God. What was the nurse thinking. She apologized later. It's not a good memory. Hard to get that picture out of my mind.

She lived for 100 years dying just a few weeks short of her 100th birthday. David, my brother, and I had made plans for a big party. Even the President of the United States sent her a birthday card.

I want my mother. I'm hurting and I still want her. I still talk to her. You see she called me every day of my life, so how couldn't I want to tell her that I was hurting?

"I'm hurting, Mom. Some of your grandkids and great-grandchildren live far away in Israel and I feel like my heart is breaking again." Or other times: "It's probably just a pinched nerve, but it's been over six months." "My foot is tingling, my calf feels like it's on fire. It's an unrelenting pain and the doctor doesn't know what it is yet."

I never told her how bad it was because I didn't want to worry her. Now in my mind I tell her everything. Years ago when I would visit her I wanted to share my pain with her but I never did.

She never knew I had back surgery, just a few weeks after she died. Spinal fusion, all those things I was missing in my body were now being replaced by something else, not tonsils, not appendix, not a left kidney, not breasts, but now six screws and six rods. Within the same week a spinal fluid leak, kind of like when you take your car in to be fixed, they always break something else. She never knew that.

Okay, so she can't really hear me now. But just maybe…

"Mother, I can't find the words to write about you. It seems I learned about you by watching you be who you were. A woman who cared about others and never said no, certainly not to me. Then that day when David said to you, "it's okay Mom, you can say or do anything you want to now. It's okay," he said, "you can stop "biting your lip."

Mom must have thought about it and now came that brand new mother. Me, her only daughter, who never had an argument or any act of rebellion or any words with her. This woman who gave or did anything I ever asked of her. Lemon meringue pies, brownies at the drop of a hat. Clothes, money, piano, bicycles, anything I wanted, even, oh, I forgot, just not that puppy I found and brought home. The perfect mother, a lady who played cards and mahjong, was beautiful, volunteered for orphaned infants at a nursery, the Douglas Park Day and Night Nursery. How did I ever remember that name, I'll never know.

Here I am living in a tiny studio apartment near Chicago. I like it, I can only sit on one chair at a time or be in one room at a time, why do I need more rooms? It's been an interesting life, yes, I've had some difficult times, and some wonderful times. That's what life is all about.

I've supported myself and managed to live an active, good, happy, giving help to others type life, just as I learned from you. "But, Mom, sometimes I still want to talk to you."

Can you hear me Mom? Can you hear me now?

S.A.S.E.

CHAPTER 20

ARTHUR / THE HONEYMOON

I was thinking about Arthur; remembering our first date.

I'm smiling now. Can you see me?

"I'm Arthur" you said, "I'm a little early. I hope that's all right."

"No problem, but I thought your name was Randy."

"My mother had trouble saying her "R's," kind of like "Ba Ba Walters" so she called me Andy. I didn't like it. So I'm Arthur."

Of course, you were kidding. You're cute, I thought. You're funny, too, but you knew you were a few years older than me. Okay, honey, you were cute, but for God's sake, you were 10 years older than me. You were 30 years old!

"But I looked so young," you said.

You did. We did have fun. I loved your sense of humor and you were so smart. Of course, I would have never said yes to our date if I had known how old you were. Except I knew my father was ten years older than my mother so I wasn't so afraid of that part, but still, ten years.

"I just kept chasing you, kept calling."

I decided not to see you again, but I kept thinking about you. I talked to my father, told him you were very nice, smart and also, kind of good-looking. "But, I'm not going to go out with him again," I told him, "no sirree, he's waay too old."

Then remember I told you what Dad asked me.

"Does he make a good living?"

"Dad, I don't know. Why would I ask him that?"

"Excuse me, is this my daughter talking? The high school cashmere sweater queen?"

"That hurts. I'm way past that and you know it."

"Maybe you might want to eat, you might want a roof over your head, and you never know, honey, you might want just one more cashmere sweater. I can't take care of you forever, you know."

"Oh, Dad," I managed to squeak out. "You're right. I do need a pink cashmere and maybe another blue one too. Hey, thanks for the offer, Dad." We laughed together.

So that day, Arthur, when you told me you loved me. I, of course, thought that meant we had to get married. I thought getting married would mean I would be able to get blue wall to wall shag carpeting in our first apartment. I wanted to get married but that carpeting was also something else I wanted. How naïve I was.

We married. I ate one radish on our wedding day because I couldn't eat much. And, the choice of a radish which could have given me (gas) was certainly not a good choice for a new bride. But, I survived even though I was very nervous getting married to a man I knew for only six months. You were almost a stranger. Yet, I did show the same strength I would need later on without you. I said no sometimes when I needed to do so. For example, I wouldn't eat the first piece of our wedding cake you were supposed to and tried to feed to me. I said no. I just didn't like it, it wasn't chocolate. Our honeymoon was a big event; my first airplane ride ever. My first everything experience. You know what I mean? I came well prepared. I had a trousseau; bridal clothes better than anyone else. It was weird. Everything had sparkly blue, green, purple and white tiny sequins that were attached to all my underwear, my two bathing suits and four night gowns. All those sequins and spangles flickered all over the carpet. When you, my new husband, turned off the lights that first night they seemed to come alive on the floor. We laughed so hard and finally the scary honeymoon became fun. At last we bonded.

My best friend, who had grown up rich and (still thought she was), took me shopping to Saks Fifth Avenue.

Joan said "you absolutely must have all these necessary things."

"What necessary things?" I asked her.

Well, let me tell you, my bride-groom, you sure seemed impressed. However, you spent many hours of our honeymoon picking up all the colorful sequins that for some unknown reason kept falling off all over the hotel rooms we stayed in. Key West, Cuba and Miami Beach honeymooners following after us into those hotel rooms, no doubt wondered about the few sparkly sequins you might have missed.

The irony is the one thing I left behind that also fell off and out of my beautiful white bathing suit, were "blow up bust pads." Yes. That's what I said, "blow up." A "straw" came inside the pads and you blew air into it and it was magic. I was then a size D instead of an A. You never knew how that happened, did you?

Hey, I sure could have used that straw later on after that first surgery. It was our first big scare where we thought I was going to die first. Instead you surprised us all by you doing that so suddenly just those few months later.

From that auspicious beginning of my first and only real marriage our four children and then our seven grandchildren came into the world. Sadly you never knew our grandkids. You know what, honey, I think, you do know. Remember, those white lights and the long tunnel so many people see...

CHAPTER 21

BOOK

Arthur, you know what else I did?

I wrote a book. It's a slightly fictionalized account of my life story, not a memoir. Why make it fiction? I knew you would ask that, you silly man. Well, my memory is so bad I was afraid I couldn't write a real memoir.

I know it's been a long time but I think of you often and sometimes I even talk to you. I hear that a lot of people do that after they've lost someone they loved and, I sure did love you, so at least I don't feel crazy.

The grief and despair that I felt are long over. Thank God, because that was tough. I worked very hard after you were gone, my fault I know. I never let you buy that life insurance policy that you wanted "just in case" as you tried to tell me. I kept saying let's live for today, why think about stuff like that, we're young.

I had some hard times with having our four kids and little money but I learned that breast cancer, kidney cancer and widowhood are survivable. At first it certainly seemed bad. Much later it became an opportunity by helping others, gaining energy, going back to school, recreating and re-inventing my life. I still do live one day at a time. I stay in the present and try not to jump ahead to the future.

I work better that way and I don't worry as much. I must say that how I want to feel or how I think I should feel and how I really feel is often very different. To try to do something is often to lie; for me it's better when I just do it.

The mourning is done now and I'm in the morning of my life. Yet, now I need noise to fall asleep since you don't play music on my back anymore. That was my best sleeping pill. Beethoven's 9th as I remember. And, yes, honey, I'm a senior citizen now, and in this, my older life, I've had a few more surgeries, got a bit of arthritis, a little heartburn, osteoporosis, high cholesterol, a few urinary tract infections, runny nose when it shouldn't be running, don't sleep through the night very often, have to get up to go to the bathroom, but I must admit, please excuse my humility, but my hair is kind of pretty. Not totally grey, not as dark as it used to be, darn, I can't think of the word it's called. Wait a minute, my senior moment is passing…hold on a minute…I just thought of it, "salt and pepper." That's right, isn't it? You always could remember a word when I asked you; you were really smart.

I seem to have a lot of that now, word finding problems, you know, forgetting words. Sort of reminds me of my mother, she had the same problem just before she passed away. I seem to have no trouble remembering way back when, but what I had for lunch today, please don't ask me.

I always remember Judy's sudden growth spurt, at about age thirteen. Suddenly, our little girl was gone. With the boys it seemed more gradual. They're all grown up now and I miss the days when we were all together. That's the way it was, the way it's supposed to be and now that is exactly how it is.

Just wanted to catch you up on who I am now because you left way too soon too soon too soon...

S.A.S.E.

EPILOGUE

The other day I got this phone call very early in the morning, about 7:00 am. I was still in bed. I didn't recognize the man's voice.

"Hello, this is Kenneth."

"Who, who did you say" I asked in my still asleep voice.

"Kenny, he said, "Kenny, this is Kenny."

"I'm sorry you have the wrong number" I told him as I started to hang up.

He quickly said, "No, it's me, Kenny from high school."

"Kenny from high school? Oh, oh, oh, wow, Kenny from High Sch… from my high school? But it's been years since we saw each other, when we graduated, so many years, how did you get my number, it's so many years…"

"I googled you."

"You what, you what? You googled me?"

"Yes, it's me Kenny, I just lost my wife, she died early this morning," he said.

"What, you what? What did you say? Your wife died just now; did you say your wife just died?

"Yes."

"Oh, my God, I'm so sorry, so very sorry. "But why are you calling me, why didn't you call 911?"

"Are you married?" this man named Kenny asked.

"What, what did you say?"

"Are you single?" this man named Kenny asked.

*

When I got up from the floor where I had landed after I fell off of my bed, I realized what and why he was asking.

It was then I knew that my name was still Anna...

But everything else was different.

THE END